MORGAN'S PATH

BY

KAREN MARIE

COLEMAN

Kaldonya Brunson
PUBLISHING

Email: authorkarencoleman@yahoo.com

Visit our official website at www.karencoleman.org

Table Of Contents

CHAPTER ONE

Morgan Foster is a fun-loving sixteen-year-old living in the wealthy town of Holbrook, California. Amid luxury homes, grand architectural buildings, and incredible landscapes, there was no shortage of fun activities for the residents of the town. On the weekends, shopping malls, amusement parks, and area lakes were filled with teens. As a rite of passage, each teen would get their car as soon as they received their driver's license. Their parents purchased pricey vehicles for them, which could be seen cruising through the city streets. Parents were in fierce competition to ensure their children were enrolled in the best academic programs and Ivy League schools. Morgan was among this elite group. Although she has a privileged lifestyle, she lives a fairly normal teen existence. She's a kind girl with a down-to-earth personality. She enjoys acting and has performed in many stage productions from age three. She often performs in her school plays and is enrolled in drama courses at the community theater just outside of town. Morgan traveled throughout America to see many productions. She and her mother make an annual trip to New York to take in several Broadway shows. In her spare time, Morgan volunteers at the Holbrook Children's Hospital. She enjoys teaching the children all she knows about acting and letting them perform small skits. The children love it, and it brightens their day. She has three of the best friends a girl could hope for:

Mackenzie Washington, Jamie Evans, and Christina Jefferson.

Mackenzie is a beautiful African American teen who's been her best friend since elementary school; they're the closest. Jamie's a red-haired, freckled-faced gossip. They don't reveal much around her for fear of her revealing their secrets. Christina's the tough, dark-haired beauty. Although she appeared tough, she was quite friendly. The teens were looking forward to their senior year. They were on the cheerleading squad in their sophomore and junior years. They had a trip planned to Spain with their school, which was a major event.

Morgan's father was away on business. He's an architect and owns the town's only architectural engineering firm. He'd designed many of the structures in the town, not to mention his many projects across the United States. He was rarely home, and Morgan's mother, who was affected by his absence, chose to spend her time shopping, having plastic surgery, and somewhat partying like a young teen. Morgan was mature and seemed more of an adult than her mother.

She loves her mother deeply; she feels she enjoys herself a little too much. She's carefree and spirited, and Morgan's friends love her. She relied more on Morgan and her friends for companionship. She seems the typical middle-class housewife, looking forty in the face and refusing to grow old gracefully. She did this by changing her greying hair to its original blonde and doing just about everything possible to look more youthful. She was beautiful before the surgeries, and no one ever noticed the changes, except for her breast implants. She's five-foot-five-foot-ten, with greyish-blue eyes, a deep bronze tan, and a thinly toned figure. Still, she sought to have more surgeries.

It was Monday morning, the first day of summer break, and Morgan was at the cosmetic surgery center with her mother, who was having yet another surgery. Morgan was a bit disappointed that she'd chosen the first day of her summer break to have the surgery, causing her to have to be there with her instead of hanging out with her friends. The nurses arrived to prep her mother for surgery. Once she was taken to the operating room, Morgan went to the family waiting area and texted her friends. After getting no response, she checked her social media pages. She saw postings of her friends at the lake. She began scrolling through their photos and commenting on their posts. After a couple of hours had passed, she was interrupted by a male nurse.

"Hello, Morgan Foster." She looked up from her phone. "Wow, he's kinda cute," she thought as she looked up at the nurse. Out of several visits to the clinic, she couldn't recall ever seeing this young man before. He looked rather young to be a nurse. He appeared to be around seventeen or eighteen years old. He could easily be mistaken for a surfer type or lifeguard rather than a nurse.

"Mrs. Foster is in the recovery room if you would like to come back, please."

"Sure."

"I'll walk you back, follow me."

She gathered her mother's things and walked to the recovery room with the nurse. On their way back, her curiosity got the better of her, and she had to ask, "Are you new here?"

"Yes, I am. This is my first month. Why do you ask?"

"I've been here several times, and this is the first time I've seen you."

Before she could stop her mouth from speaking, she blurted out, "How old are you?" She was thinking about the question, but it slipped out.

He laughed and said, "I know I look young to be a nurse. Actually, I'm almost thirty years old."

She was embarrassed. He could see her cheeks turn red. "I'm sorry," she said.

"No, don't worry about it. I get it all the time."

They finally made it to the recovery room. Her mother's head was wrapped in large bandages. Another nurse there was disconnecting her IV. She was awake but a bit drowsy. She saw Morgan come inside.

"Hey sweetheart, I finally got that out of the way. How do I look?"

She looked at her mother and smiled. "You look great mom. People will think we're sisters." Her mother looked at her and reached out her hand for Morgan's.

"See, that's why I love you. You can cheer me up no matter what the case may be." She knew Morgan was lying to her because of the many bandages on her face. The nurse looked at her mother and said, "Mrs. Foster, I'm sure you're going to look just as beautiful as always."

Morgan said, "I'm sure she will. I tell her often that she doesn't need the surgeries, but it makes her happy." She looked at the nurse and smiled. The doctor walked into the room and spoke with her mother about her aftercare. Still dressed in his scrubs, which looked somewhat stylish on him with his slender muscular arms and firm body, his handsome ruddy face donned a friendly smile as he entered. He walked over to her bedside and examined her bandages.

"Mrs. Foster, your surgery went great. I want you to keep the bandages on today. I'll see you back here tomorrow so I can remove them. I've sent your prescription to your pharmacy; you may pick it up when you're ready. You'll need to take one for pain with food and no alcohol please." Morgan looked on as the handsome older doctor spoke with her mother. Morgan knew from past experiences with her mother that she wasn't going to obey the doctor's instructions. Dr. Collins was aware of this as well.

Her mother looked at him and said, "I will Doctor Collins."

The doctor then turned his attention toward Morgan and said, "Morgan, keep an eye on her for me, okay." He shook Morgan's hand.

"I'll try, but you know mom does what she wants."

"Mrs. Foster, have a wonderful afternoon. I'll see you back here tomorrow."

Morgan helped the nurse walk her mother to a waiting wheelchair, and she was wheeled to the car. They got her medication and drove home. They pulled up to the large two-story Mediterranean-styled home. She tapped the horn for their housekeeper Munsey to come and help with her mother. While Morgan was helping her mother, Munsey was removing the things from the car. Morgan helped her mother into her bedroom. As she peeled the comforter down to help her get into bed, she noticed her mother already picking at her bandages. She looked at her with pursed lips and said, "Mom, stop pulling at the bandages."

"Oh honey, I want to see what it looks like."

"Mom, you heard what the doctor said. Leave them on for now. You always do this and get upset because it looks bad. You end up panicking and calling the doctor. Just leave them alone. He'll remove them tomorrow in his office."

Her mother exhaled and took her daughter's hand, which she had extended to help her in bed. She leaned her head back on her pillow. "Morgan, you worry too much honey."

"You leave me no choice, Mom. You should follow the doctor's instructions. Whatever he tells you to do, you seem to do the exact opposite. He told me to make sure you do as he says."

Morgan began fixing the comforter around her mother as she lay back in bed. "Can you have Munsey bring me a drink?" Morgan looked at her mother with a slight frown on her face.

"Mom, you're not supposed to drink alcohol with your pain pills. I swear you act as if you're the daughter instead of the mother."

"Just do as I tell you, darling; anyway, how many times do I have to tell you that it helps to soothe me, and I feel much better?"

She shook her head at her mother and called for Munsey as she was told. Morgan was indifferent to the many plastic surgeries her mother would have, and they were becoming the norm for her. With each surgery, her mother insisted that she go along with her. She was missing out on fun with her friends. Her friends were already at the lake and would probably be gone by the time she arrived. She stood in the window of her mother's large bedroom, looking out over the grounds. The noonday sun was shining through the window, causing a glow in her blonde hair.

Morgan sighed as she thought of the fun her friends were having without her. She noticed Munsey had walked into the room with drinks on a tray. Morgan was relieved to see her. She smiled at Morgan and gave a nodding gesture, releasing her from her duties of helping her mom. Morgan returned the smile and slipped away quietly while her mother was distracted. Munsey gave her the drink; she took her medicine and drifted off to sleep.

Helen Munsey is their live-in housekeeper. She has been with the Foster family since Morgan was a toddler. She helped to care for her while her mother completed her schooling. Since her father was always away, having a live-in housekeeper was beneficial to the home. Munsey never married. She was in her early forties when she came to live with the Fosters. She's considered a member of the family.

Morgan's father built her a small home by the guest house on the back of their property. She represented a sense of stability and was a shoulder to lean on if Morgan ever needed it. Everyone in the home relied on her practical wisdom and willingness to listen. She was a great friend, and they loved her dearly.

Morgan finally got settled and was taking a relaxing moment to herself. Suddenly, she heard a scream coming from her mother's room. She dropped what she was doing and ran to see what the matter was. "Mom, what's wrong?"

Her mother was looking in the mirror at her face. "Look at me. Look at my face. Wait until I get my hands on that doctor."

"Mom, I told you it's supposed to look that way. The swelling will go down in a few days."

"But look at me! I have two black eyes. It looks like I've been hit in the face with a frying pan. I want to cry, but my eyes hurt so much, and tears burn my skin."

Munsey rushed into the room. She saw Mrs. Foster making a fuss. She calmed her. Munsey convinced her not to call the doctor, and she repeated what Morgan had told her.

"Mrs. Foster, you're going to look beautiful when the bruising and the swelling go down. Nobody knows you better than Dr. Collins; he always does a fabulous job. That's why you chose him. You are his masterpiece. Why if I ever thought about getting some work done, I would choose him."

Morgan added, "Mom, you're going to look great. They continued talking to her. Munsey helped to add more gauze and she and Morgan quietly talked to each other until her mother went to sleep. Morgan went to their indoor pool. She put her earbuds in her ears and turned the volume up on her cell phone. She exhaled and leaned back looking at the sky through the glass skylight. Munsey came in to check on her. She touched her on the shoulder to get her attention. Morgan popped the earbuds out of her ears.

"Morgan darling, can I get you anything?"

"No, thank you Munsey."

"Okay, let me know when you're ready," She noticed Morgan wasn't her normal self, so she asked, "Is everything okay?"

Looking a little somber, Morgan said, "Yeah, I'm okay. I was looking forward to spending time with my friends today, but mom needs me, so I have to be here."

"A young girl *should* be out enjoying time with her friends."

"I don't want to sound heartless Munsey, but I wish dad or somebody else were here to help with mom. She insists on me doing everything with her. I have my own friends, and I want to spend time with them. I don't want to have to always be at the doctor's office or whatever she's doing these days. I think she needs more friends."

14

Munsey looked at her sympathetically, with large brown eyes and a beautiful brown face. She knew all too well what Morgan was going through. She, too, had had to compensate for Mrs. Foster's lack of friends, and she often put off her chores to comfort, console, or just lend an ear. "Dear, I understand. Why don't you go and find them? I'll take care of your mother."

"Nah, she'll just call my cell phone and find a reason for me to come home."

"It'll be okay, go on and hang out with your friends."

"Are you sure?"

"Yes, I'm sure, now go."

Morgan put her bathing suit on under her clothes and called her friends. They were still at the lake. The teens loved the lake rather than going to the country club to swim, citing too many rules and stipulations. They were freer at the lake and could enjoy themselves. She got her paddle board and paddle and placed them in the jeep. She put an extra board in the jeep and left. She could see the cars of all her friends and one bright red sports car parked in the grass off to itself. When she pulled her vehicle up to the lake, her three friends, Jamie, Mackenzie, and Christina, ran to her car. They each took turns hugging her. She noticed her friend Mackenzie's hair. "Wow, Mackenzie, you got braids."

"Yes, I did. I got them done last night. Do you like them?"

"I think they're very nice."

"I had to come up with something if I'm going to be at the lake for the summer. Besides, it's easier to manage this way."

Christina said, "It's about time you decided to join us. How's your mom doing?"

"She's doing fine. Munsey is taking care of her now. I was so glad she stepped up. If she hadn't, I don't think I could've come today."

Mackenzie said, "That would've been a tragedy, too, because look who's here!" Morgan looked up and noticed the well-tanned, dark-haired football player Logan Sparks. He began attending their school in his junior year. Before that, he was enrolled in a boys' only private school. Logan has shown much interest in Morgan in the year he met her. She enjoys the fact that he's attracted to her, and although the feeling is mutual, she has no plans to date him. At least, that's what she tells her friends. She glanced his way smiling shyly. He flashed a quick smile and waved. She looked at her friends a little embarrassed that they were watching. Jamie had a mile-wide smile on her freckled face. She bumped Morgan's shoulder and said, "Morgan, you know you like him. Why don't you go ahead and go out with him?"

"I don't know. I've not given it much thought, and you shouldn't either; now let's go swimming." Morgan snatched her top off and pulled her shorts off. She wore a fuchsia two-piece swimsuit underneath. She kicked her flip-flops from her feet, and they all ran and jumped in the lake. They weren't in the water for five minutes before Logan swam over.

"Hi Morgan," he said.

She smiled coyly and said, "Hi."

Waving his arms and keeping his body afloat, he said, "I was hoping to see you today." With beads of water dripping from her hair and face, she lifted her head for a second, trying to catch her breath. Her heart was racing. She thought it would jump out of her chest. With her eyes locked on his, she said under her breath, "He is so cute," Still taken with her captivating beauty, he said,

"Morgan, you're really beautiful." She wasn't ready to respond. Instead, she playfully splashed water in his face. He laughed and slapped the water, causing water to splash on her. She swam away. He quickly followed her, engaging in a playful game of cat and mouse. She screamed when she looked behind her and noticed he was gaining an edge on her. She swam to the edge of the lake and jumped out of the water with Logan still in pursuit. When he caught up with her, he grabbed her and tickled her. She laughed uncontrollably while begging him to stop. They both fell on the grass on their backs laughing. He lay

17

on his side, resting his head on his hand, and stared at her. He followed her on social media and interacted with her often. She was much more lovely in person. He was a true fan of hers. He watched as her skin began to dry in the beaming sunlight. She cut her eyes at him, still laughing.

"Morgan, are you ever going to go out with me? I've been asking you for a while, but you've never given me an answer. Do you have a boyfriend that I don't know about?"

She sat up and pulled her knees to her chest. She wrapped her arms around her legs, resting her chin on her knees. "No, I'm not dating anyone. Tell me, why should I go out with you?"

"Because I like you. I think you're a wonderful girl, and I love being around you. You're kind, and you're very pretty. You know I could stare at you forever. Do you remember when we were in the school play together, and we kissed? I still remember. It was a short one, but it was a kiss, nonetheless. You know I've been to your last three stage performances this year? You're talented, beautiful, and smart."

"Thank you, Logan. I don't remember seeing you in the audience at any of my performances."

"I was there."

"So, you like the theater?"

"Yes, I do. It's not something I'd like everyone to know. I mean, if the guys knew that the star quarterback was into that sort of thing, they would have a crack at my expense."

"That's silly," she said. "I wouldn't care what others thought of me."

"You know guys can be a bit harsh. They're still teasing me about wearing those tights in the Romeo and Juliet play, but I'd wear them again if I could kiss you again."

He focused his attention on her. The roaring of the jet skis and the laughter of their friends faded in the background as their eyes met. She could tell he desired to kiss her at the moment. As he leaned in closer, Morgan realized that she simply wasn't ready for the kiss, at least not before the first date. A little nervous, she blurted out, "I brought my paddle board. Did you bring one?"

"Nah; that's a hundred-thousand-dollar sports car. It's not equipped for lugging around lake gear."

"Well, I brought an extra board. Would you like to use it?"

"Perhaps in a few minutes. Let's talk a little more. This is the first chance I've gotten to be alone with you. I want to get to know a little more about you.

She realized he was really into her, and it may not have been a simple crush. They talked for about thirty minutes. She noticed they shared similar interests. After giving it a little more thought, she said, "You know, I think it would be nice if we went out at least for one date. When would you like to go?"

He was excited upon hearing that she would go out with him. "How about tomorrow evening? Do you have any plans?"

"Well, my mom had surgery today, and I've been helping her, but can I get back to you and let you know for sure?"

"Sure."

Morgan stood to her feet and playfully pushed him. With Logan's help, she went to her vehicle and got the boards. She jumped in the water, got on her board, and paddled over to her friends. Although her day started as a bummer, she was finally able to enjoy it. To top it off, she had a date soon. She couldn't have been happier.

The evening had come, and the sun was setting. Morgan said goodbyes to her friends and went home. After a full, eventful day, she was exhausted.

Munsey had dinner ready, just like clockwork. Morgan showered, then ate her dinner. She plopped her body on her bed. As soon as her head hit the pillow, she heard her name being called. She placed her pillow over her head as if it could make the voice stop. "Morgan, come here please." Feeling annoyed, she jumped from her bed and hurried to her mother's bedroom.

"I'm coming, Mom," she yelled. She walked in. Her mother was lying on her back in a lounging position.

"Honey, can you please hand me my pain pills? I need a little bit of water, too."

Morgan exhaled. "Yes Mom."

"Thank you dear." Her mother noticed she seemed a bit irritated. Trying to make small talk, she asked, "How was your day? Munsey told me you went to the lake."

"It was nice to be with my friends. I enjoyed my day."

"Morgan, sweetheart, I want to thank you for going with me today to the clinic. You don't know how much it meant to me to have you there. I'm sorry for asking you for so much. Munsey and I talked earlier, and she seems to think that I've been putting too much on you. She reminded me of what it's like to be a teen. I understand your disappointment in spending your day caring for me, especially on your summer break. You've worked hard all year, and you should enjoy your break. It's yours, and I have no right to infringe on that. Munsey will take care of things here. That's what she's hired to do."

Morgan listened to her mother as she went on. She almost felt a sense of guilt. Had she been selfish in not wanting to be with her mother that day? Was it that obvious, she thought? She got the bottle of pills from her mother's nightstand and poured a glass of water from the pitcher that was left there by Munsey. She placed the pill on her mother's lip. She then placed the straw in her mouth so she could take a sip of water. She put the glass on the nightstand and helped her mother lay back and relax. She lay on the bed next to her.

"Mom, I love you. I don't mind helping you. You know that. It's just that I was looking forward to spending the day with my friends. It was all we talked about. I must admit, I was a bit disappointed that I had to sit in the clinic this morning, but I'm glad I went. I'm also glad you're okay. Whenever you need me, you know I'm always going to be here for you. You're my mom." She reached for her mother's hand and held it tight. Her mom tried to smile, but her face ached. She looked at Morgan trying to move her head as little as possible.

"I know I ask too much of you. Your dad is always away, and I have no real life, so I guess I have you make up for it. It's wrong of me to ask you to give up your social life because I don't have one."

"Mom, you have a wonderful social life. You have plenty of friends."

"What friends? If you're talking about those ladies at the country club, I don't care to be around them all that much. Other than the fact we all have wealth; we have nothing else in common. They lie, gossip, and cheat on their husbands and they think it's okay. That's not me. I love your father, and honesty *is* one of my greater qualities. I try to find other things that interest me, but I can't seem to find my niche. Being a mother is all I know, and I've managed to turn that into a co-dependent relationship."

"Mom please, don't talk like that. Yes, you may be a handful at times, but that's how you are. There's nothing wrong with wanting to spend time with family." Morgan wanted to lighten the mood. She didn't want to discuss the topic anymore, so she changed the subject.

"I have a date this week."

"Really, with whom may I ask?"

"With this guy named Logan Sparks. He attends my school. He's the one who played Romeo in the school play."

"Oh yeah, I remember him. He's cute."

"Yes, he's very cute. My friends think so too. He has a head full of thick dark hair, and tanned muscles. He has the neatest smile. Most of the girls at school have a crush on him. I think he likes me."

Her mom interrupted her. "Of course, he likes you. How could he not? You're gorgeous." Morgan continued,

"He's been trying to get me to go out with him for a while now. I wasn't too sure at first, but after seeing him at the lake today, I decided to give it a shot. It's just one date though. If he's nice and if things work out, perhaps we can go out again."

"So, where is he taking you on this date?"

"I'm not sure. I told him I would contact him. We'll talk more about it. I think he wants to surprise me with something nice."

"That's nice dear," her mom said in a drowsy voice. "Just be home at a decent hour."

"Alright, Mom. I never go past curfew." Her mother half-yawned, trying not to cause pain to her face.

"I love you Morgan." Her mother drifted off to sleep. Morgan was too tired to go into her bedroom, so she went to sleep beside her mother.

The following morning…

Morgan was awakened by Munsey coming into the room to bring her mother breakfast. She watched her as she placed the tray of food at her mother's bedside. She used the remote to open the large drapes allowing the sunshine in. "Morgan, would you like your breakfast in here with your mother, or will you eat in the dining room?" Before she could answer, she heard a familiar voice yelling,

"Yoo-hoo, where is everybody? Excited, Morgan sprinted from the bed. The voice continued. "Morgan, Claire, where is everybody?" Morgan heard high-heeled shoes clacking on the hardwood floors. "Where is everybody? Hello?"

"We're in here Edy," said Morgan's mother. Before Morgan could make it to the door, her aunt Edith walked in.

"So, it looks like the party's in here," Edith said. Morgan greeted her.

"Aunt Edy. It's good to see you. I missed you." She squeezed her aunt tightly around the waist.

"Morgan, let her breathe. You're going to squeeze the life out of her."

"Hello Claire. Look at you. What have you had done now?" Edith asked.

"A little nip and tuck."

"If you keep going to that plastic surgeon, pretty soon there won't be much left of your face." She walked over to the bed and held her sister's hand. Morgan followed.

"So, Aunt Edy, how long are you going to be in Holbrook?"

"I'm going to be here for a few weeks."

"Will you be staying with us?"

"Yes, where else would I stay?"

"I'm so glad you'll be here; I have a lot I want to tell you."

"When I get settled in, I want to hear all about it."

"Can I get you something to eat Edith?" Munsey asked.

"I'm going to come down in a minute and grab a bite."

"Morgan, are you eating in here?"

"I'm going to eat with Aunt Edy."

Morgan's aunt Edith was Claire's younger sister by seven years. Besides her mother and Mackenzie, Morgan's Aunt Edith was her favorite person. They shared a closeness that words couldn't describe. Morgan confides in her telling her things she can't or won't discuss with her mother or her close friends. Her aunt is one with an open heart and mind, and she gives Morgan sound advice without making her feel bad. They discuss everything from relationships to fashions, and anything personal they could share. Her aunt is the one who talked with her about sex and other issues concerning teen girls. She's more of a best friend. Morgan feels free when she's around. Edith's a fun aunt and she loves spoiling her niece. With no kids of her own, she had taken Morgan under her wing. While her aunt visited with her mother, Morgan went to her room, showered, and got dressed, then went to the dining room for breakfast. She couldn't wait to tell her aunt about her upcoming date with Logan and other events that involved her life.

Morgan walked into the dining area where Edith was already enjoying a cup of coffee. She looked over at the designer purse and the cute shoes she was wearing. Her aunt loved fashion almost as much as she did. Munsey was busy working and bringing condiments to the dining table. She placed several platters before them, one with fresh fruit, croissants, and muffins, and two more with traditional breakfast meats consisting of sausage, bacon, and ham. She placed the eating utensils within their reach. Morgan was hungry so she grabbed a strip of bacon and stuffed it in her mouth as if it was her last meal. "Slow down Morgan. Nobody's gonna steal it from you. There's plenty of food. By the way; you're punishing that bacon." Morgan laughed. She settled in her seat. She took a plate, got a fork, and placed her food on her plate.

"I see you're letting your hair grow out," her aunt said looking at Morgan's long hair. "It's very pretty."

"Thank you. It's not as pretty as yours."

"That's not true. You have lovely hair."

"Aunt Edy, you're so beautiful."

"So are you. You look like your aunt Edith. Everyone knows that. Morgan smiled at the thought of looking like a woman so beautiful. Not only was she a beautiful woman, but she was also intelligent. She was single, stylish, and classy; and made a name for herself in the business world. Morgan hoped to be like her when she got older. "What have you been up to since I've been gone?" Edith asked.

"Nothing really, just life as usual. I had a great year. I'm advancing in all my classes. Because we've done so well this year, our social studies teacher planned a trip to Spain for those of us who earned the highest test scores. We're so excited. I've acted in several stage performances, including the Shakespeare play at school. I sent you the video for that one. I have a few more videos that I want to watch with you."

"I would love to see them. You are a great actor. You'll go on to do shows on Broadway, or better still, have an amazing acting career."

"Well, I don't know about that," Morgan said bashfully.

"I never have to worry about you because you're a top-notch kid. You're talented and smart, kinda like your aunt. You know they say talent skips a generation. I guess that explains your mother." They both laughed.

"I'm just kidding. Don't tell her I said that. It's our secret." Munsey was walking around them making a small fuss to ensure they were pleased with their meal. Wanting to spend quality time with Morgan, her aunt suggested they eat their breakfast by the indoor pool, away from earshot of anyone. "I have an idea, let's go and eat by the pool." They gathered their food and sat poolside.

"So, about this trip to Spain, can you tell me more about it?"

"Yes, we've been studying the culture in class. We've learned so much. I'm excited to be experiencing it in person. All my friends will be going, and I think it's going to be awesome. Even Logan Sparks is going."

Her aunt smiled and said, "Logan Sparks, who is that?"

"He's only the hottest guy in school, and he happens to have a crush on me."

"You seem surprised that he would like you. Have you looked in the mirror lately? You're gorgeous and you're a very sweet person. Any guy would be lucky if you looked their way."

"Well, he's been asking me out for a while. He asked my friends about me. He's been trying to get them to convince me to go out with him. Yesterday he was at the lake, and he asked me again. This time I agreed. I mean he's cute and all, but I wasn't really into him all that much. Most of the girls like him and I guess I can kinda see why. I think he's funny in a goofy kind of way. I guess I pictured him as this annoying jock by the way he strutted around the school. Then he drives this loud, flashy, red sports car, so I thought he may have been stuck on himself. After having a conversation with him, he doesn't seem so bad. We're in the same social studies class. Since he was at the lake yesterday, we swam and talked about a lot of stuff. Since acting in our school play, that was our first time interacting on a personal level. Usually, we only speak in the hallways in passing. We have several things in common. I'm looking forward to our date."

"Well, I hope you have fun. It's good to see you so happy. Tell me, how are you and your mother getting along? Is she still a pain in the rear?"

Morgan chuckled. "Of course she is, but you know that's just mom. She's lonely because Dad is always away. When I was little, I was her personal little project. We've always been close. Now that I'm older and I have my own friends, I think she feels as if I no longer need her. I do, just not in the same way as I did back then. She's been the den mother to all my friends for years carrying us to recitals, cheerleading practice, volleyball games, and doing just about everything for all of us. My friends love her as if she was their mom. I love spending time with her, but I wanted to enjoy the lake with my friends. Since dad was at work, no one else was available to drive her home from her surgery. She wanted me here to help her yesterday and I didn't mind, but I had been looking forward to my summer break. Munsey took over for me."

"I'm glad you got a chance to go. I'll have a chat with your mom."

"Thank you, but I'm not sure it'll help. Besides she's cool." Morgan changed the subject.

So, Aunt Edy, have you found a guy yet?"

"Who says I'm looking?"

"I just thought that since the last guy didn't work out too well, you would find someone else who could make you happy."

"Morgan honey, I don't need a guy to make me happy. I'm already happy. I enjoy my life either way.

Besides, I date sometimes. I'm not missing out on anything. I'm more focused on my career right now. That's the reason I'm in town. I have an important meeting with a company here in Holbrook, and they're offering me a major contract. It's a pretty lucrative deal and I'm excited about the prospect. I've worked hard in school, went to a great college, and now all that hard work has been paying off in the form of many lucrative offers."

"Well, I'm glad you're here."

While they were speaking, Morgan's mother interrupted them by calling her name. Edith shook her head and pursed her lips. "Oh Lord, this lady here is something else. I'll go and see what she needs." Morgan stayed to eat her breakfast while her aunt went to check on her mother. She walked into the room and asked.

"What is it, sis?"

"I need my pain pills," she said.

"Where are they?" Edith asked.

They're over on the nightstand. They should be on a platter next to a small pitcher of water. Edith found the pills and gave them to her.

"How much pain are you in?"

"I feel a little pressure around my eyelids, and I have a headache." Edith helped her by passing her the pills. "I need help getting in the shower Edy. I have to go to the doctor today." After taking her pain pills, Edith helped her get dressed.

"Claire, why do you keep doing this to yourself?" she asked.

"I do it because I like the results I'm getting."

"How many surgeries have you had so far?"

"I've had six."

"Do you plan on getting anything else done?"

"I don't know, I might."

"Well, remember the example you're setting for your daughter."

"What do my surgeries have to do with Morgan? I don't think I'm doing anything wrong. I'm enjoying my life, and this is what I want. To tell you the truth, you could use a little work yourself, perhaps get some enhancements."

"I'm fine. I don't need any work done. I'm happy with how God made me. I don't define my beauty by society's standards. Claire, you're a lovely woman. All those surgeries could possibly have long-term negative effects."

Feeling a bit annoyed at her sister's questions, Claire looked at her with a slight frown and asked, "Hey what gives? Why are you being so negative about this?"

"I love you, Claire. I just hope you're not having these surgeries to compensate for other things going on in your life. I've heard once you start having work done, you get addicted to it. Then you have poor little Morgan running you back and forth to these surgeries and taking care of you as if she's a nurse. She's a teenager and she should be allowed to do what teens love to do. That means not being cooped up in here taking care of her mother who chooses to have multiple surgeries. If you choose to keep doing this to yourself, then at least hire a nurse and stop stealing Morgan's life from her. She told me she almost missed out on hanging out with her friends because of you. Allow her to be free and stop monopolizing all her time. Just because she's willing to do everything for you, doesn't mean you should take advantage of her. You're even overworking Munsey. You need to get a life and get some friends of your own."

Claire exhaled slowly and tried to look up at her sister. Although still in pain she said, "I hear what you're saying, Edy. Munsey spoke with me about that too. I love Morgan. I admit I've been a bit much these past few years. Peter's always away, and Morgan no longer needs me. I get lonely sometimes. I tried hanging out with the ladies at the club, but we have nothing in common. I don't like them. All I ever know is how to be a wife and mother. I feel that no one needs me now. I don't know what to do with myself."

"Well, having unnecessary surgeries won't make things better. Find a hobby; something that you're interested in. For example, you have several degrees that you've never used. Look into putting them to use. You may feel as if you don't need to work, so you may want to volunteer your time to help someone else. You used to love making jewelry, and you were quite good at it. Why not do that? Since you love fashion, take some sewing classes. Do something, but at least get out of this house and enjoy your life. What are you going to do when Morgan leaves for college or gets married and has a family of her own? You've got to let her go now or you're going to make matters worse for the both of you, then she'll end up resenting you."

"I know Edy, but it's just so hard to let go. I'll work on it." Edith got Claire's purse and drove her to her doctor's appointment."

Morgan was on the phone with her friend Mackenzie. She lived across the street from Morgan. Mackenzie's mother is a skilled heart surgeon. She often performs surgeries at the Holbrook Hospital, where Morgan volunteers. Mackenzie's father is the president of the large corporation, that her grandfather started. Both Mackenzie and Morgan were born in Holbrook, and they shared the same birthday month, which is October.

Mackenzie drove her car across the street to Morgan's home. Morgan was still curling her hair. Her friend walked into her room and sat in the large plush turquoise chair next to her bed.

"Morgan, I still love this chair," she said as she eased her tiny body into it. She kicked her feet up and looked at her phone. "Do you need my help?" she asked Morgan.

"No, I just have one more to go and I'll be ready." "Hey, grab my bag over there on the other side of the bed for me."

"Okay," she said. "You know Jamie wants to ride with us to the mall, so we'll stop by and pick her up. She called as soon as I got off the phone with you. You don't mind, do you?" Mackenzie asked hoping she'd say yes. She had already told Jamie they would pick her up. Initially, it was supposed to be just the two of them.

"Of course not, that means we can't talk about anything juicy because she loves to tell everything she hears."

"She *is* a blabbermouth, isn't she?"

"Yep"

They both giggled.

Once Morgan was ready, the girls hopped in Mackenzie's little burgundy Lexus, and left for the mall. While on the way, Logan called Morgan. When she looked at the caller ID, she let out a loud scream. Mackenzie slammed the brakes and said, "Girl, don't scream like that while I'm driving. You scared me."

In her excitement, Morgan said, "It's Logan Sparks." Excited, Mackenzie screamed too.

"Answer it girl, but don't act excited."

"Okay." Morgan calmed herself and answered the call.

"Hello."

"Hey, Morgan, it's Logan."

"Hi, Logan," she said, smiling and looking at her friend.

"What's up?"

"Just riding to the mall with Mackenzie."

"Okay, cool, how long will y'all be at the mall?"

"Probably for a couple of hours. We'll be shopping, and then we're going to get something to eat while we're there."

"Do you think you'll be able to go out with me this weekend, maybe Friday or Saturday?"

"We can go out on Friday. Mackenzie and I have plans on Saturday."

"Alright, I'll come and get you around seven. Will that be okay?"

"Can you come around six-thirty? My curfew is ten-thirty so that'll give us time to catch a movie or dinner perhaps, or whatever it is we want to do."

"Yes, I can come at that time."

He hesitated as if he wanted to say something else. Morgan waited to hear what he would say next. After a moment of silence, he asked, "Would you mind if I call you sometimes just to talk?"

"Sure, that'll be fine," she said. He lingered on the phone a little longer.

"Well, I gotta go, Logan. We're pulling up at Jamie's house, and it's going to get noisy, but I'll talk to you later."

"Okay; bye."

She ended the call and looked at her friend. She screamed again and did a happy dance in her seat.

"So, what'd he say girl?" Mackenzie asked.

"He wants to take me out on Friday evening."

"Awesome. I'm so glad you finally said yes. Girl, that boy has had a crush on you for the longest time. He's never dated any of the girls at school. All he asks about is you. Since you agreed to go out with him, have him take you somewhere fancy. You know I'll never go out with a boy if he can't take me to the finest restaurants. Don't let him take you to some cheap place you can go to with your friends. He's got the money. His dad is extremely rich. The whole town knows that. They own one of the largest banks in Holbrook. Also, he should bring you an expensive gift. With the money they have, he can afford it."

"You *would* say that, Mackenzie. You're so lavish. While it's true that I love nice things; my dad has plenty of money as well. I don't need a guy to buy me things. If I want something, all I have to do is ask my daddy, and he'll get it for me."

"But they're supposed to spend money on you, especially if they want to date you. My mom says so."

"Mackenzie, you date guys you don't even like simply because they're rich. Then you break up with them and keep their gifts."

"I know, right? I'm bad, huh!" Mackenzie laughed.

"This is just a date. I'm sure he'll take me someplace nice. I just want to get to know him and have fun."

"Well, make sure he pays; don't pull your credit card out for anything." Morgan laughed and brushed off her comment. They pulled into Jamie's driveway. She got into the car, and they went to the mall.

They shopped until they were hungry, so they went to the food court. As they were eating, Mackenzie looked up and saw Logan walking by. Mackenzie said, "Girl, is that Logan?" Morgan looked up and saw him walking by, but she wasn't sure if it was him.

"It sure looked like him," Morgan said. They continued with their meal. After they ate, they went into a few more stores. When they were coming out, they bumped into Logan.

"Hello ladies," he said, looking at Morgan. She smiled and said, "I thought I saw you earlier. I wasn't sure. What are you doing here?"

"I want to look presentable for our date, so I stopped by to grab myself something to wear. I won't be here long."

"Okay."

"How much longer are you all going to be here?" he asked.

"We're getting ready to leave."

"So, are you going home?"

"I'm not sure; we're just hanging out. We may go and sit by the lake or go back to my place."

"Okay, have fun. It would've been nice if you and I could've gone riding out by the pier; that would be fun, don't you think?"

Mackenzie looked at her and nudged her, "That sounds like a great idea. Besides, I'm exhausted from all that shopping. I'm ready to go home and relax. Jamie and I will watch a few movies. We'll find something to do."

"I was looking forward to the rest of the evening with you guys," Morgan told her.

Logan said, "You *should* be with your friends."

"We can always hang out anytime," Mackenzie said. She looked at Morgan urging her to go with Logan. "Are you sure?" she asked.

"Yes, I'm sure. Now go and enjoy yourself."

Morgan looked at Logan and said, "I guess it's me and you."

They went to find something for him to wear for their date. Afterward, he put the top down on his car, and they went riding around town. He took her home around six-thirty. She enjoyed the thought of possibly seeing more of him.

CHAPTER TWO

It was Wednesday morning. Morgan slept in until around nine-forty-five. She finally opened her eyes and immediately thought about the day before. She had a pleasant smile on her face. She got her cell phone to look at the time. She noticed she had several missed calls; two were from Mackenzie, one from Jamie, and four from Logan. She called Mackenzie who was eager to hear how the evening went between her and Logan. After she was done talking to her, she called Jamie. They chatted for about fifteen minutes until her phone beeped. It was Logan calling her again.

"Jamie, I gotta go. I have another caller."

"Okay, call me later girl," said Jamie.

"I will," Morgan said. She answered the other line.

"Hello,"

"Good morning Morgan."

"Good morning."

"How are you this morning?"

"I'm doing okay; I'm a bit sleepy. I'm just now waking up."

"I thought of you last night," he said.

She smiled. "I thought about you too."

"Hey, I have something for you. Step outside"

"You're outside?"

"Yes, get dressed and come out."

"But I look a mess. I haven't even showered or brushed my teeth."

"Aww, that doesn't matter. Step outside."

She was a bit surprised to know he was outside her home. She ran to the restroom and brushed her teeth and then her hair. She went to the front door and looked outside; sure enough, he was in the driveway. He got out of his car with a bouquet of roses and a white Teddy bear. The bear had a nice diamond necklace around its neck. He handed her the gifts.

"Oh my! Logan, this is so nice." She took in the aroma of the roses. "The roses smell great. Aww, the bear is so cute. Oh wow, is that a diamond necklace?"

"It sure is. Turn around, and let me put it on you." She turned around and lifted her long blonde hair from her shoulders and whipped it up. He placed the necklace around her neck and kissed her on the cheek.

"Thank you, Logan. I love it," she said, admiring the expensive necklace.

"You're welcome," he said. He leaned back on his car, with folded arms, and said, "I would love for you to have lunch with me today. Can you make some time for that?"

"I have plans. I'm spending time with my aunt today."

"Oh, okay, when you're done with her, can we hang out?"

"Yes, I'm sure we can." He talked with her for about an hour in the driveway, hoping she would ask him to come inside. She told him she had to go. She wanted to get ready for her day. He reluctantly left and she went inside to spend time with her family. Munsey saw her as she walked back inside. She noticed the roses and the bear.

"Very nice gifts. Looks like you have an admirer."

"Thank you, Munsey. It seems as if I do." Morgan smiled and walked past her. She went into her bedroom. Her aunt Edith came in just as she was placing her gifts on her computer desk.

"Hmm, what do you have there, Morgan?"

"It's nothing really, just a little something from a friend."

"Would it happen to be from the young man you were telling me about, a handsome Mr. Logan?"

She looked at her aunt with a bashful smile. "Yes, it is."

"He seems like a thoughtful young man. It's very nice of him to bring you gifts. The roses are lovely."

"Look at the necklace he bought me."

"Very nice. Wait a minute, let me see that," her aunt said taking a closer look at the necklace.

"Morgan sweetie, this is a real diamond necklace!"

"I noticed that. Isn't it beautiful?"

"It sure is, and very expensive too. Now, how long have you known this young man?"

"I've known him for about a year, but we're going on our first date Friday."

"Sweetie, you may want to think twice before accepting such an expensive gift like this, especially since you guys are just starting your friendship."

"Well, my friend Mackenzie said, boys are supposed to buy nice things for girls they like. She gets lots of amazing gifts all the time."

"Yeah, about that. Sweetie, you shouldn't accept expensive gifts from someone too soon. You can't rightly know their motives for giving you the gift. I'm not saying what he's done for you isn't thoughtful, but you really must be careful when accepting gifts, especially early on in a friendship. That looks like a fifteen-thousand-dollar necklace. People tend to only give those types of gifts when they're in a long-term, committed relationship. So be cautious about that. If he tries to give you any more expensive gifts, hold off on taking them until you get to know him a little better, even still watch yourself. When will you see him again?"

"He wanted to spend the day with me, but I told him I was going to spend the day with you."

"Are you going?"

"No, I want us to have our girl's day out. I'm looking forward to spending time with you."

"That's so sweet of you. You don't have to waste your time with an old girl like me. Enjoy your summer with your friends. As I told you, I'm here on business. I'm not here to interfere with your life."

"Aunt Edy, you're not interfering. I want to spend time with you. Besides, you'll have to help me pick out something nice for my date. It'll be so much fun. Now I'm about to get dressed. I'm expecting you to be ready so we can go on our normal outing." Edith chuckled and said, "Yes ma'am." She was pleased to hear that her young niece wanted to spend time with her. Before Morgan got dressed, she checked in on her mother. Doctor Collins had removed her bandages. She was still in pain.

"Good morning, Mom."

"Morning sweetheart. You slept in a little late this morning, didn't you?"

"Yes, I spent yesterday at the mall with Mackenzie and Jamie, and then Logan and I went riding and listening to music. When I came inside, you were already asleep, and I was exhausted, so I went straight to sleep."

"It must've been an exciting evening."

"It was. I just came to tell you that Aunt Edy and I are hanging out today. Is there something I can do for you?" Her mother smiled as much as she could without pain, "No Morgan. You go and enjoy your day."

"Okay, mom. I'll be back soon. I love you."

"Love you too."

Morgan and her aunt went shopping. Afterward, they went to the Holbrook Country Club for lunch. Logan called her several times while they were out. She told him she was having lunch at the country club and told him she would call him soon. She and her aunt were laughing and talking when she looked up and noticed Logan had walked in. He was seated by the hostess across from where they were sitting. Morgan waved at him. He smiled and waved back. She motioned for him to come over. He took his water and walked over to the table.

"Aunt Edy, this is my friend Logan Sparks. Logan, this is my Aunt Edith." Logan put his hand out to shake hers, and with a slight head nod, he said, "It's nice to meet you, ma'am. Morgan, you look lovely today. Your hair looks so pretty, but I noticed you're not wearing the necklace I bought you."

"I'm saving it to wear for our date. I chose this necklace because it goes with what I'm wearing today." He gave her a dry smile. Her aunt noticed it, and it made her uncomfortable.

"Logan, how old are you?" she asked. "I'm seventeen years old."

"What grade are you in?"

"I'm in the twelfth grade when school starts, the same as Morgan."

"Do you have college plans?"

"Yes, then afterward, I planned on working with my dad. I want to make a great life for myself so that my wife will have the best when I get married." He cut his eyes at Morgan.

Edith said, "Isn't it a little too soon for you to be thinking about marriage?"

"No, I don't think so; you should always plan years ahead."

"I think you should enjoy being a teen for now and think about the heavy stuff later."

"We're all entitled to our opinions," he scoffed. "My parents were married just out of high school, and they're successful, and they're still together." He touched Morgan's hand and said, "So, Morgan, what will you be doing later on?"

Edith answered for her, "She and I have plans," "Well, what are you doing after you and your aunt are finished with your plans?"

"I'm not sure," said Morgan.

"Call me; it would be nice to get together," he said. He stood to his feet and said, "It was nice to meet you, ma'am. I'll see you soon Morgan."

Morgan smiled and said, "Okay. I'll call you later." Logan left the club. Edith looked at Morgan and said, "So that's Logan Sparks. Do you really like him?"

"I think I do."

"Well, watch yourself. Try not to date just one person. Keep your options open. Have fun, and don't take things too seriously. You're young, and you should enjoy life now. You have your entire future ahead of you, and you don't have to be bogged down with heavy distractions."

"Alright, Aunt Edy." They went on to enjoy a spa day filled with beauty treatments from head to toe. Morgan went home and spent time with her mother. Her aunt joined them. They watched classic movies. Her mother nodded off. Munsey walked in and said, "Morgan, I think your cell phone is ringing. It's been ringing for a while now. Would you like me to bring it to you?"

"No, Munsey. I'll get it." Morgan got her phone and saw six missed calls, all from Logan. She called him back.

"Hello," she said, curious as to why he had called so many times.

"Hi Morgan. I thought you said you were going to call me."

"I was planning on it. I'm still spending time with my family. Since my mother can't do much, we're hanging out with her and keeping her company. I'll call you as soon as I'm done."

"Well, wait. Before you go, I'd like to know if you'd like to hang out this evening."

"Not tonight. I'm going to stay in with my family; besides, my aunt is only here for a few weeks, and she'll be gone again. We always spend time together when she's here. I'll call you before I go to bed, though."

"Okay, well I'll be waiting for your call," he said. Morgan ended the call and went back with her mother and aunt.

"Okay, I'm back what did I miss?"

"Not much, I'll play back to where we were before you left," her aunt said.

The home was quiet as they were watching TV. Munsey was finished with her chores. Morgan heard her nickname being called. "Angel!"

"Dad!" she shrieked.

She ran towards his voice. She was excited as if he'd been gone for months. He planted his feet firmly on the floor and stood his six-foot frame solid anticipating her jumping in his arms. Seeing his daughter's cheerful greeting warmed his heart. He may have been tired from his travels, but she gave him a fresh burst of energy. He held his arms out for her. After hugging him, she grabbed the handle of his briefcase and wheeled it into his office. He followed her. "How was work this week?" she asked. "Work was work," he said as he combed his fingers through his tawny brown hair. He loosened his tie. "Hey Angel, I almost forgot, I bought you a little something." Her dad always brought nice things home from his travels for Morgan and her mother. He reached into his jacket pocket to retrieve her gift. She jumped up and down clapping her hands like a little girl, her ponytail bopping as she jumped.

"What is it, Daddy?"

"Open it and see." She snatched the box out of his hands and opened it.

"Oh my gosh, Daddy, diamond earrings! The ones I wanted. How did you know?"

"Well, those not-so-subtle hints you kept giving me. You know, the one where you left the magazine in my lap, as I slept in my recliner with a circle around them and a note saying, "I like these, Daddy.""

She giggled. "I love them, Dad. You're awesome." She immediately put them on.

"Hey Angel, your tire is flat out there. I'll call someone to come and fix it for you. You must have run over a nail or a piece of glass. If you need to go somewhere, you take my car."

"I'm not going anywhere tonight." She kissed her dad's cheek. She followed him into the bedroom where her aunt and mother were. He looked at his wife who was reclining in the bed. She was happy to see him.

"Hello Peter."

"Well, if it isn't the bride of Frankenstein." He gave a hearty laugh. His voice carried throughout the room. He loved teasing her. He was quite a jokester.

"Peter, stop teasing me," she said.

"What babe? Besides my handsome looks and amazing body, you said my sense of humor is one of the reasons you were attracted to me."

"But not when you're teasing me." He sat beside his wife on the bed. He took her hand and kissed it. "I *would* kiss your forehead, but I can't find an available spot." She hit at him.

"Stop it Peter."

He smiled and said, "I missed you, darling."

"Me too," she said.

He looked at his sister-in-law. "Hello there, Edy; how are ya?"

"I'm doing quite well Peter."

"It's good to see you. Are you gonna keep your sister here out of trouble?"

"I'll see what I can do, but I think she's a lost cause." She and Peter laughed.

"Not you too Eddy," Claire said.

"Aww sis, I'm just kidding. You know I love you."

"Mom, look what dad bought me." Morgan showed her mother and her aunt her new earrings.

"They're beautiful dear," her mother said.

Morgan and her aunt gathered their things and left the room to give her parents their privacy. Her aunt said, "Morgan honey, I'm going to call it a night. I'm going to get a nice warm bath and get some rest. I have things to do tomorrow."

"Alright Aunt Eddy. Good night." Morgan went into her bedroom and closed her door. She called Logan and they talked until she fell asleep.

CHAPTER THREE

It was Friday and Morgan was getting ready for her date with Logan. She had been talking with him all week and seemed to like the direction their friendship was going. She put on a nice sleek black miniskirt with a gorgeous midriff pink top. She pulled her hair into a stylish ponytail. She placed the necklace Logan had given her on her neck and wore the diamond earrings her father gave her. Her father was in his office on his computer. She tried stepping over the sketches that were lying on the floor and every available space. After walking in she said, "Dad, how do I look?"

"Angel, you look beautiful. Where are you going?"

"I have a date this evening."

"You have a date? What's his name?"

"His name is Logan Sparks."

"Sparks; Hmmm… His family owns the Reliable Banks of Holbrook?"

"Yes, daddy."

"Is he a nice boy?"

"Yes, and he's handsome and thoughtful too. He brought me roses, a nice bear, and this lovely necklace. Do you like it?"

"It's nice. What time is he coming to pick you up?"

"He'll be here in a few minutes."

"That's great; I would love to meet him."

"Okay, I can't wait for you to meet him. You're going to like him."

"We'll see," he said. Morgan went to her room. Her cell phone rang. It was Logan calling.

"Hey Morgan, I'm outside."

"Logan, my dad is home, and he wants to meet you."

"Your father wants to meet me? We don't have time. I've made reservations and I don't want to be late."

"It'll only take a few minutes. Come on inside." Morgan told her dad that he was there. She went to the door and let Logan in. She smiled when she saw him. His dark hair was styled professionally. He was dressed in a nice pair of olive-colored dressy slacks, a light green shirt, and an olive-colored tie.

"You look very handsome Logan. You smell nice too," she said.

"You're very beautiful Morgan." Her dad was standing behind her. "Come on in and meet my dad." She introduced them. Logan gave a firm handshake and smiled. "It's an honor to meet you, Mr. Foster."

"It's nice meeting you, Logan."

They sat and talked for about ten minutes. Afterward, they were allowed to leave. When they got in the car, he looked at her and said, "Morgan those are nice earrings. They look expensive. Where'd you get them?"

"My dad bought them for me. I've always wanted a pair. Do you like them?"

"I think they're nice. I like your hair down. I think you look much prettier that way." He reached for her ponytail and let her hair down. He styled it with his fingers.

"Now you look amazing."

"Thank you," she said. He took her to an upscale restaurant. When they were seated, the server came over to take their drink order. After they ordered their drinks, they looked at their menus. She saw what she wanted, and she said, "I want the lobster bisque, the filet mignon, and a salad." As she named her meal, a look of disapproval showed on Logan's face. "You're going to get fat if you eat all that food. I think you need to eat something light in calories." When the server arrived to take their order, he proceeded to order for them both. She was a bit disappointed because he didn't allow her to pick what she truly wanted. For her, he ordered grilled salmon, with roasted vegetables and a light salad. She didn't necessarily like what he ordered for her, but she ate it anyway. Since he knew she enjoyed the theater, he managed to get the last two tickets to a major production in the next town. Afterward, they took a slow walk along the boardwalk by the pier. He showered her with affection, and he doted on her. Over the next few weeks, they were dating non-stop. They were always together. She was spending less time with her family and friends and more time with Logan. Her aunt was staying a little longer because she found a few more clients in town. She rented a tiny townhouse against her sister's wishes. They begged her to stay in the guest house, but she was entertaining potential clients, and she didn't want to be a burden to her sister. She was expected to be in Holbrook for the next six months. Morgan's father was back working. Her mother was doing better. She was busying herself with designing jewelry. She created exclusive pieces from broaches and earrings to necklaces and bracelets. She took her sister Edith's advice and took sewing classes. She knew the basics of sewing and had already made several garments as a hobby. This time she was committed to her craft. She began to design her own clothes incorporating some of the jewelry into the fabrics of the garments she was creating. She was such a natural at it. People in the town took notice and they began asking her to design pieces for them. She was amazed at the attention her jewelry was getting. When her husband realized how well her business was taking off, he purchased her a nice boutique in the town shopping center

58

and had it redesigned to fit her needs. He spared no expense. The grand opening brought in hundreds of people eager to see the place. She finally got all her things moved in, and she was working daily.

It was Saturday afternoon, and Morgan was driving home from an audition for the lead role in the Shakespeare production. It was the same theater that Logan had taken her to on their first official date. She was nervous during her audition, but she recited her lines with total perfection. She felt she'd made a good impression on the judges. Feeling great vibes from their reaction to her performance, she hoped she would land the part. She went home and relaxed from her busy week. She was finally getting a free moment away from Logan. Mackenzie noticed she was home, so she stopped by. When Morgan went to the door to let her inside, Mackenzie said, "Girl, where have you been? I miss my best friend. We don't hang out anymore. It's all about you and Logan."

"I know. I think I'm falling in love with him. He's so special. He treats me like a queen. He says he loves everything about me. He buys me clothes and jewelry and he takes good care of me."

"I'm happy for you girl, but we miss spending time with you. Pretty soon school will start, and we won't be able to do all the fun things we said we'd do together. You've spent your entire summer with Logan."

"Mackenzie, I promise to take some time for us. We'll make plans to do something fun," Morgan said.

"Morgan, the last few times we tried that, Logan showed up every time and took you away with him. He always pops up when you're with your friends."

"Logan has always done that ever since we've known him. You know that. Besides, you're the one who insisted that I go out with him."

"I'm not hating on you or anything like that; it's just that I would like to spend time with you without him always popping up."

"I promise I'm gonna make time for us. It'll just be us."

Doubting her, Mackenzie smiled and said, "Okay, I'm going to remember you said that." Morgan wanted a snack, so she called for Munsey.

"Yes dear, what do you need?"

"Munsey, can you make us some cheese sticks and potato skins?"

"I can make you a nice lunch if you want baby."

"No, we just want a few appetizers. I'm not that hungry." Munsey fixed the girls a snack, and Morgan filled her friend in on all she had been up to over the past few weeks. Mackenzie snapped a few photos of her and

Morgan and posted them on her page. After posting her photos, she noticed that Morgan had been tagged in some of Logan's pictures. She said, "Girl, Logan has tagged you in a gang of pictures. He changed his relationship status to *"In a relationship with Morgan Foster."* I see he's proud of you."

Morgan opened her laptop and logged into her social media account. She noticed the pictures that Logan had added. She was puzzled because they never discussed her being his girlfriend. She was taking her aunt's advice to take it slow. She liked him, but he hadn't officially asked her to be his girlfriend. She was sure to talk to him about it as soon as she saw him again. She untagged herself in the posts and closed her computer. Her phone rang immediately.

"Hello."

"Hello Morgan, what's going on?"

"Nothing, just here with Mackenzie."

"I noticed you were just online, and you removed the tags on the pictures I posted."

"Yes, I did. We haven't discussed our relationship status yet."

"I didn't think we had to. Everyone knows you're my girl."

"Really, well I didn't know it."

"Well, I'm telling you now; you're my girl so I've changed it and added the tags."

"Please don't do that, Logan."

Morgan logged back into her page and noticed he added the tags. She closed her account until she and Logan could talk more about their relationship. She and Mackenzie went riding for a while. When she arrived home, she noticed Logan sitting in her driveway. "Well, there he is again. I told you we can't do anything together without him showing up," Mackenzie said out of frustration. Morgan was a little annoyed that he was at her home.

"Mackenzie, I'll call you later."

"Sure you will. Logan is here, so I know that's not gonna happen."

"Cut me some slack, will ya?"

"I'm sorry," Mackenzie said. She hugged her, and she drove away. Morgan walked up to Logan, who was standing outside his car.

"Logan, why are you here?" she asked.

"We need to talk."

"I don't feel like talking right now."

"I want to apologize to you. You're right. I had no right to change my status without speaking with you first."

"Yeah, you should've discussed it with me. I don't like that."

"Well, are you ashamed of me?"

"No, I'm not. Don't do anything to my page or tag me in pictures without my consent."

"I'm sorry it won't happen again." He looked at her and smiled. He pulled her close to him and kissed her. "I have something for you."

"Really, what is it?"

He opened the passenger door of his car. "Get in," he said. She got in. He went around on the driver's side and got in. He opened the glove compartment and pulled out a small bag from a jewelry store. He gave her the bag. She was excited.

"What's inside?" she asked. She opened it and saw a beautiful solitaire diamond ring.

"Logan, this is nice, but I can't accept it."

"Yes, you can. I want you to be my girlfriend."

"Really?"

"I like you very much. We've been seeing each other for a while now; it just makes sense for you to be my girlfriend."

"I guess so," she said. He took the ring and placed it on her finger. It was a perfect fit. They kissed. She invited him inside for a while to watch television with her.

Making it official

Morgan, her mother, and her aunt Edith went to church together. Her mother made a large meal for them to celebrate Morgan landing the lead role in the play. She invited Mackenzie, Logan, Jamie, and her other friend Christina over to eat and hang by the pool. Mackenzie brought a male friend with her. At the dinner table, Logan sat next to Morgan. He stared at her the entire dinner as she laughed with her friends. She enjoyed their company because she hadn't spent much time with them. She was happy they were there. They were discussing their summer activities. Logan often interrupted her, wanting all her attention.

Her aunt Edith noticed his obsessive behavior. She wasn't pleased with it in the least. She kept her eyes on him the entire time he was there. After dinner, the teens sat poolside and laughed and played around. Morgan put on a pair of shorts and a bathing suit top. Her friends did the same. Logan saw her and became furious. He said, "Morgan, you need to put something else on. You know I don't think it's appropriate for you to be half naked in front of other guys."

"Chill out Logan, it's only a bathing suit. We're by the pool." He gritted his teeth in anger and grabbed her by the arm. He squeezed her arm very tight and said, "Change now."

Mackenzie yelled at him. "Logan let go of her arm."

Morgan interrupted her and said, "It's okay Mackenzie. I'll change. It's no problem." She went into her room and put on a top. Mackenzie followed her.

"Morgan, why is he putting his hands on you?"

"It's no big deal," she said.

"Yes, it is. He shouldn't be touching you like that."

"Shhh. You're going to make things worse. Just shut up about it. Besides, it didn't hurt."

"Morgan, you need to tell your parents."

"Just leave it alone."

They went back to the pool.

"That's better," Logan said.

Mackenzie was angry with him. She sat and stared at him, trying to make eye contact, but he wouldn't look at her. He could feel the heated stares come from her direction. Morgan sat next to him. He held her hand. Everyone else was wading in the pool, laughing and enjoying themselves, while Morgan looked on. She wanted to join them so badly but didn't want to upset Logan. It seemed as if he didn't want her to mix and mingle with her friends.

Jamie said, "Morgan, why don't you guys come and swim with us."

"We're okay," Logan said.

"You guys are no fun," she said.

Her friends went on enjoying themselves.

After everyone had gone home for the evening, Morgan went to her room and noticed that her arm was bruising. She sat at the edge of her bed and cried a little. She was hurting inside. She took out a little jewelry box containing eyebrow razors and other sharp utensils. She went into her bathroom, sat in her tub, and proceeded to cut herself on her inner thigh. She took some alcohol and poured it on the cuts. She sat there in the tub and cried for about an hour.

Logan called her and apologized for being so rough with her. He planned a date with her the following evening. He said it would be special, and he told her what to wear. She did as she was told, and he stopped by to pick her up. He took her to the town's most lavish hotel. His father rented it for him. He told his dad that he and a few friends he wanted to hang out with. When they made it to the room, he ordered room service for them. After the food arrived, they ate. He poured himself a little liquor he had taken from his dad's liquor cabinet.

"Are you drinking alcohol?" she asked.

"Sure, I'm going to pour you a glass too."

"I'm sorry, but I don't drink. I'm only sixteen. You're seventeen. You shouldn't be drinking either. Where did you get alcohol?"

"I brought it from home. Here, drink some." He tried to force the liquor on her.

"I can't stand the taste or smell," she said, turning her head.

Logan drank the entire glass of bourbon. I brought you here because I think it's time for us to make our relationship official. He took Morgan's hand and led her to the bedroom area of the suite. He kissed her. She didn't like the taste of alcohol on his lips. She turned her head slightly. He forced a kiss on her. She didn't want to fight with him. He put his hands inside hers and forcefully pulled her closer. He kissed her again. She gagged at the smell of liquor on his breath. She watched as he took his clothes off. He was down to his underwear.

"What are you doing Logan?" she asked.

"I want to make love to you. It's about time we take our relationship to the next level."

"I'm not ready for sex. I want to wait until I'm married."

"Technically, we're going to be married anyway, so let's make love."

"I'm not getting married until after I've finished college. There is no guarantee that we will even be together by then." He pulled her by the arm and tried to touch her body.

"No Logan, I'm not going to have sex with you."

"Why do you think I brought you here? I've spent all this money on you. I've bought you clothes, jewelry, and many other gifts. I've spent thousands of dollars on you. You're my girlfriend, and I want to make love to you."

"You only bought those things as a way of apologizing to me after you hit me. Are you saying I owe you sex for everything you've done for me? I can buy my own things, you know. My daddy is just as wealthy as yours." He was angered by her comment. He took pride in the fact that his parents had money. He thought he could buy and sell people or use his father's money to control others. Morgan was right, her father was very wealthy, too, and she didn't need him for anything, and he hated that.

"I'm not going to have sex with you because I'm not ready," she said.

"Morgan, you're going to stop acting like a baby and make love to me."

The brute male slammed her to the bed. He then climbed atop her. She pushed him off. He slapped her face hard. He pinned her to the bed and tried to remove her underwear. She kneed him in the groin. He punched her repeatedly, as he had done so many times before. At the beginning of the friendship, it was just pushing and shoving. It soon escalated to more hitting. He beats her almost every day. He was doing it again. She screamed with each blow that landed on her head and facial area. As she covered her head, he beat her on her arms and back. She tried to leave, but he wouldn't allow her to go. She reached for her cell phone to call for help, but he snatched it from her and broke it. She ran to the upper level of the suite to get away from him. He quickly followed her. After catching her, he yelled in her ear.

"I hate when you make me like this. You're always making me angry. I'm just about tired of you, Morgan. You go around town flaunting yourself for other guys with your short shorts, skimpy mini-skirts, and halters. Yeah, I've been watching you for a while now. You think I'm going to let another guy have you, but I'm not. If I can't have you, then nobody will. Then there's your friend Mackenzie, who brings guys by to look at you. I don't like that. Oh, and I want you to drop out of the Shakespeare production. You're my girl, and I won't have you kissing another guy."

Although she was afraid of him, she was livid at his mere suggestion to ask her to drop out of the play. "Logan I've worked extremely hard, and I earned that role. It's something I've always wanted to do. I'm not dropping out of the play. How could you ask me to do that?"

She could hear the rage in his voice. His face was unrecognizable, as his anger seemed to escalate. "I'm not going to tell you again." Morgan was trembling and trying to find a way to escape. He took her by her arm and forcefully sat her on the sofa and made her sit and listen to him as he berated her. He then told her that she had to perform oral sex on him. She was afraid because of all she had already been through that evening. She felt intimidated by him. Fearful for her safety, she complied with his demands. After about an hour of drama, he knew he had to take her home. He began to calm down. As he sobered, he took her hand.

"I'm sorry for hitting you. I said I wouldn't hit you again, but sometimes you make me angry. I gotta tell you what to wear, what to eat. I mean, you don't seem to get it. I bring you here tonight for a nice romantic evening, and you act ungrateful."

She listened without saying a word. She didn't want to anger him more. All she wanted at this point was to make it home safe. He held her and cried. He sobbed like a baby. She comforted him, although she was the one who needed to be consoled. "I'm so sorry, baby. I promise I won't let it happen again. Please trust me," he said. She knew he was lying. He had made this promise many times before. Pretending to listen, she took his hands and placed them in hers. She looked him in the eyes and said,

"I believe you." She held him tight. This was to calm him until she could get away safely. Afterward, she went to the restroom, washed her face, and rinsed her mouth. She was very hurt by what had taken place. His abuse now included sexual assault, and she was truly devastated. She cried in the restroom. He called for her to come out so he could take her home. He got dressed, and they left. She silently sobbed the whole ride home.

She hoped nobody was in the living room when she made it home. She didn't want to have to explain her bruises. When she opened the entry door, she noticed her mom and aunt were in the living room working and watching television. She rushed past them so they wouldn't notice how distraught she was. She went into her room and immediately took all her clothes off. She looked at her body and saw the bruising on her neck and chest area. She had a large handprint on her face from where Logan slapped her. Her Aunt Edith, sensing something wasn't right, knew it was unlike her to walk past her and not speak. Normally, Morgan was a vibrant, bubbly, friendly girl. Her aunt wanted to know what was going on with her. She walked into Morgan's bedroom without knocking. She was disturbed by what she was witnessing. She saw Morgan with an eyebrow razor, and she was cutting herself on her inner thigh. Morgan didn't notice her aunt when she walked in. When her aunt noticed all the bruises on her body, she was speechless. She immediately ran to her niece's side and grabbed her wrist. "Morgan, stop it! What are you doing to yourself? What happened to you? …. And who put all these bruises on you?"

Morgan looked up at her aunt, who had tears in her eyes. "Please don't tell mom."

"Morgan, you know I have to tell her."

"If you do, you'll only make it worse," Aunt Edy.

Her aunt went to the restroom, got a towel, and placed it on her thigh. Morgan hadn't cut deep enough to bleed, but Edith could tell that she had been doing this by the old scars.

"Morgan, talk to me. Tell me what's going on with you. Why are you harming yourself?"

"It makes me feel better. It takes away the pain I'm feeling inside."

"What happened tonight? Is that Logan boy hitting you?"

"He doesn't mean to. He just gets upset sometimes. It's mostly my fault."

"Look at me, Morgan. It's never your fault when someone hits you. It's their fault. You don't deserve to be abused. Nobody does. How long has this been going on?"

"It started two weeks after we began dating. He gets upset because I choose to hang out with my friends instead of going out with him. Every time I want to hang out with you or anyone, he fights me. If I choose not to be with him, he always finds me and forces me to leave with him. After a while of him embarrassing me, I just stopped making plans and hung out with him. Each time he fights me, he buys me things to make up for it. Tonight, he took me to a hotel. He wanted to have a nice romantic evening. He said he wanted to make our relationship official and insisted that we make love. I told him I wasn't ready for sex. He got angry and began punching me. Aunt Edy, he forced me to…." She couldn't get the words out. "It's okay, baby," she said, hugging her. Morgan took in a burst of air and said, "He forced me to perform oral sex on him. It was horrible." Her aunt Edith was furious, and it showed, but she held her composure as she could see that Morgan wanted to spill all her secrets. She couldn't help her by losing her cool. She patiently listened as Morgan continued. "He accused me of flirting with other guys, and he says I love dressing like a whore when I'm around them. He tells me what to eat and drink, and he buys clothes that he says are appropriate for me. He even said I couldn't take the part in the Shakespeare play, and he wants me to drop out of it. I can't do that Aunt Edy. After all of it was over, he said he loves me, and that he's going to stop hitting me."

"Sweetie, you're not in a healthy relationship. I could tell he was bad news when he showed up while you and I were eating lunch. He was pushy and had an obnoxious attitude. I noticed him at the dinner table too, the way he kept glaring at you as you laughed with your friends. He's no good for you, and he has a serious problem. I had a guy like that. That's why I broke it off with him. He was too possessive. I didn't like his company, so I ended the relationship. I'm not afraid of being alone. I'd much rather be alone and happy than allow some guy to cause me misery. That means you must love yourself more than the drama others try to bring into your space. This is your life, and you only get one.

You shouldn't spend it by allowing some loser to waste your time and drain your spirit.

You're young, and you have a lot of life in you. Enjoy your life, your family, and your friends. No one should dictate to you how you should think or feel. Some people are unhappy, hurt from their past, or insecure, and they heap their problems on others. They appear to be normal, and they appear to be kind and genuine.

If you find yourself in a relationship or friendship that makes you uncomfortable, you should get out immediately. Remove yourself at the first sign of trouble. Don't try to wait it out, thinking it will get better. It won't. It never does. No one has the right to put their hands on you or heap abusive pain on you. They should never try and force you to do anything without your consent. You shouldn't feel bullied or pressured into doing anything you're uncomfortable with, and you don't have to try to please some selfish jerk who cares nothing about you. Logan's probably gotten away with it so much, that he's used to doing it. He won't change. The police will have to stop him.

He makes you feel bad about yourself with subtle put-downs and then sly remarks about your appearance to get you to feel a little insecure about yourself. He then isolates you from family and friends, that way, you're no longer under their protection. Next is brainwashing. You get sucked into a cycle that is hard to break. You must free yourself and expose your abuser. Weaken his power over you. He's a sick coward who preys on others to feel better about himself. He thinks he's strong, but a person who is unable to control their emotions is truly weak indeed. He tries to strike fear in you, but he's the one who's afraid. He doesn't feel as though he deserves you, and he's afraid he'll lose you to somebody who does. That's why he bullies you into staying with him."

Morgan looked at her aunt. It was like she was living inside her head. Everything her aunt mentioned, she realized Logan had done to her. Morgan liked Logan, but she had hope that he would stop hitting her. She missed her old life with her friends. She felt trapped in her own body because she felt she couldn't tell her parents what was happening to her. She was deathly afraid that Mackenzie was going to mention what she saw at the pool. She began cutting almost immediately after the abuse started. It was a release mechanism for her. In a way, she was relieved to be sharing her story with her aunt, but she did not want her parents to find out.

"Aunt Edy, please don't tell my parents about this."

"Sweetie, a crime has been committed against you. You've been beaten and sexually assaulted, and you're closed up in your bedroom, hurting yourself. Your parents need to know that. You need professional help, and Logan needs to get help, too. When a crime has been committed against a child, and an adult finds out about it, they are mandated by law to report the crime. I'm sorry, but I have to say something. Everything's going to be okay. We're here to help. Now I'm going to call your mother, okay?"

"Aunt Edy, please don't tell Mom."

"I'm not. I'm going to have you tell her in your way."

Morgan was afraid. She was afraid that things would get much worse if her parents got involved.

Her aunt stood to her feet and called her mother. "Claire, come here, please."

Morgan burst into tears. Her aunt held her until her mother came in. She was crying with her. Her mother walked in as they were both crying.

"What's wrong guys? Morgan, what's wrong sweetheart? Why are you crying?"

Her aunt looked at her and said, "Morgan has been having some trouble, and she needs someone to talk to about it."

"Darling, tell me what's wrong, please."

Morgan couldn't find the words to tell her mother. Her aunt helped her.

"Morgan is having some trouble with Logan."

"What kind of trouble?"

"He's been hitting her." Look at her back and take a closer look at her face. Her mother stared at the bruises in horror.

"He's hitting you? Oh sweetie, why didn't you tell us? Oh, my baby." She reached out to Morgan. She held her tightly and sobbed.

"I didn't say anything because I was afraid. He said if I ever told anyone, he would burn down your store and would hurt my family." Seeing her mother's response, she finally felt free enough to tell her everything. They couldn't believe the abuse she'd suffered at the hands of Logan. He beat her and sexually assaulted her. He held her in a prison of fear, threatening her family, and friends if she ever tried to leave him or reveal the abuse. At last, when she finished telling them about her issues with Logan, her aunt said, "There's more. Morgan has been hurting herself."

Her mother looked at her sister, confused. "What do you mean she's hurting herself?"

"She cuts herself. Honey, show your mother." Morgan reluctantly removed the towel from her thigh. Her mother gasped in disbelief. Tears streamed from Morgan's face. All of them were in tears by now.

"How could this happen? You're such a happy child. Don't worry, we're going to get help. We'll find you a great doctor.

"Mom, I don't want to see a doctor."

"We have to take you. Also, I need to call the authorities about Logan's assaults."

Morgan's mother took her to the hospital to have her examined. Edith rode along, comforting Morgan in the back seat. They notified the police on the way. An officer was sent to take the report. After leaving the hospital, Morgan's mother and aunt stayed with her all night to comfort her. Her mother called her father to fill him in on the incident. He flew home immediately to look after his daughter. The following morning, Morgan and her mother went to purchase another cell phone, but she kept the same number. Her mother also made an appointment for her to see an adolescent psychologist. His name was Dr. Neil Callahan. Morgan walked into the clinic with her parents. Her father was holding her hand. He looked at her sympathetically. He knew she was nervous and could tell she had been suffering.

"We're here for you honey. Everything is going to be okay. You're going to make it through this. We're going to do it together as a family." Morgan nodded her head without saying a word. They were called into Dr. Callahan's office. She didn't know what to expect. His office didn't look anything like the ones she saw on television shows, where the shrink sits in a chair, while the patient lies on the couch and tells all their soul. There was a large-screen television, video games, and teen-friendly magazines. There was a large seating area for families and there were four large recliners. The office was beautiful, inviting, and comfortable. She breathed a sigh of relief. She didn't want to be labeled with the stigma of being nuts. The embarrassment of having to see a shrink was more than she could take. The doctor was well-groomed and dressed in a nice suit and tie. He didn't look like a psychiatrist in the least.

"Hello Morgan. It's nice to meet you. I'm Dr. Neil Callahan. Your parents didn't tell me I would be seeing such a beautiful young fashion model. How long have you been working in that field?"

She smiled and said, "It's nice to meet you, Dr. Callahan. I'm not a model, though."

"You're one lovely young lady. Are you sure she's not a fashion model?" he said playfully posing the question to her parents. He joked and chatted with her causing her to laugh. She didn't feel so bad after meeting him. "Please, have a seat." They were all seated and Dr. Callahan spoke to them as a family unit.

Afterward, he asked Morgan to go with his aide while he spoke to her parents. She and the aide talked about everything from the latest fashions to music. This distraction kept her mind off her problems until the doctor could see her. After Dr. Callahan spoke with her parents alone, he brought Morgan in. He spoke with her about her interests and other general questions. He didn't get to her problems right away. He wanted her to open up when she was ready. If he were to help her, he knew he had to gain her trust. His approach worked, and she began to tell him what she felt comfortable sharing. She didn't start with the cutting issue right away. She discussed how she missed her friends and how she felt isolated from them. She expressed that she liked Logan, but she was fearful he would reject her if she didn't do as he told her. The doctor listened without interrupting. He didn't judge her, and he didn't try to solve her problems. He simply allowed her to vent. After speaking with him, she immediately felt better. He discussed some ways for her to deal with her emotions. When their meeting was over, he called her parents in. He didn't mention to them what Morgan shared with him.

"I've spoken with Morgan, and we discussed what she could do to cope with her emotional pain rather than *Cutting* or *Self-injury*. Cutting is extremely dangerous. It isn't necessarily a suicide attempt, but it is Morgan's way of coping with pain. For most people who choose to cut, it gives a sense of instant relief, but it creates long-term problems. We're going to implement different ways for her to deal with emotional pain. Each time you're upset or find yourself wanting to cut, I want you to get a journal and write what you're feeling. Perhaps you can take a walk or run. Speak with your parents. Tell someone you trust. You need to know you're not alone. I want you to come to see me once a week. If you feel you need to speak with me before your appointment, feel free to give me a call. Mom and Dad, for Morgan to get better, it's going to take a team effort. You must be diligent. She can work through this, and she says she's expressed a willingness to do so."

Dr. Callahan spoke more with them. On the way home, Morgan felt relieved. She felt safe because her parents knew what she had been suffering, and she no longer felt alone. She had been so afraid of them finding out. She couldn't believe the feeling of freedom she felt from them knowing and helping her. She was ready to do the work, and she was ready for the healing process to begin.

CHAPTER FOUR

Morgan's mother was like a mother hen. She wanted to watch every move she made. She was afraid to let her out of her sight, but the doctor suggested that she give her space and not smother her. She was concerned that perhaps she would injure herself severely and she wouldn't be able to save her in time. Morgan asked permission to go with Mackenzie for the day. Her mother allowed it, but she was certainly reluctant. She felt it was too soon for her to be out in public. Morgan drove to her friend's home, and they enjoyed their day as they did before Logan came into the picture.

In the meantime, Logan had been arrested. His father bailed him out. He was released and given a court date to appear on the domestic battery and the sexual assault charge. An order of protection had been served against him, and he was ordered to stay away from Morgan and her family.

He didn't know how to live without Morgan. He began following her and stalking her and her friends. He watched every move she made even though he was ordered to stay away from her. He was insanely jealous as he watched her hang out with her friends and the rest of the guys from school. She was doing her best to heal from her past and move on, but not Logan. He was busy thinking of ways to win her back. He couldn't understand how she could be so happy without him. He thought to himself, *"She acts as if she doesn't miss me at all."* He sent her a message on her social media page. He noticed she marked single as her relationship status. He sent her more messages. Frustrated that she was ignoring him, he called her inside the messenger app. Then he called her cell phone once more. "Morgan, please respond. I love you. I'm sorry for hurting you. Won't you please give me a chance to show you how much I love you? I'm not the same person I was before. I've changed."

Morgan finally got tired of him calling, and she answered the phone out of frustration.

"Logan, please don't call my phone anymore. It's over between us. You need to move on with your life."

"No Morgan. I can't live without you. I need you in my life. I'll never hit you again. I promise."

"Logan, I'm supposed to call the police if you contact me. Please don't call me or try to contact me again."

He began yelling on the phone. "I love you Morgan. I can't live without you. I'll kill myself if I can't have you. It'll be your fault. Do you want that on your conscience?"

She was undaunted by his comments. She said, "I have to go, Logan." She ended the call. He called back. She let it go to voicemail. She turned her phone off. Morgan was tempted to get upset and cut herself, but she went to her parents instead and told them about the phone call. Her mother called the wireless company and got her number changed. She contacted the police and gave them the information. Morgan continued with her life as usual. Summer break was almost over, and the school year was about to begin. It was time for everyone to register. Everyone was excited about the new school year. Morgan and her friends all rode together to sign up and get their lockers. Afterward, the twelfth-grade students agreed to meet up at the local burger stand. The word spread quickly. When Morgan and her friends showed up at the burger stand, they saw flyers on buildings and strewn about the parking lot, and each person there had one. It was a picture of Morgan, and under her image was the statement, *"Morgan Foster is a slut. She's easy and will sleep with anyone for money; just name your price."* The letter went on to describe the sexual contact that was made between Logan and Morgan, and it was graphic. When Morgan saw it, she was horrified. She knew it was Logan because of the way he described the scene from the hotel room that fateful night. She burst into tears and ran to her car. Mackenzie yelled her name. "Morgan, wait! Please, don't leave." She frantically jumped in her vehicle and drove home, almost hitting several cars in the parking lot on the way out. She cried all the way home.

Her friends tried to follow her, but she was speeding. They slowed their speed and drove to her home. Morgan made it to her driveway. She fled from her car and ran inside. She went into her room and got her case with her blades and cutting utensils. She cut herself randomly, making gashes in her skin. This time, she didn't try to hide the cuts. She screamed and yelled and cut until she was so bloody that she couldn't recognize her own arm. She fell to the floor. Munsey heard all the commotion. She called Morgan, but she didn't answer. She bumped the door with her body while rapidly hitting it.

"Morgan, are you okay? Answer me. Morgan! Answer me." Munsey stepped back, and with one firm kick, the door opened. Morgan was on the floor in a daze but conscious. Munsey tried to stop the bleeding and called the paramedics. She called Morgan's parents. Mackenzie and Jamie were outside, ringing the doorbell. As Munsey allowed the paramedics in, the girls followed them inside. They looked on as the first responders were rendering aid to their friend. Mackenzie showed Munsey the flyer and explained to her what had her upset. Morgan was taken to the hospital. Her friends followed the ambulance. Mackenzie was afraid that Morgan wasn't going to make it. She cried and prayed. Jamie did the same. Morgan's mother and her aunt arrived at the hospital. By the time they made it, the doctors had already stitched up her wounds. Distraught, her mother ran to her bedside. "Morgan baby, are you okay? I knew I shouldn't have let you out of my sight. Why did you do this to yourself? You were doing so well. What happened?"

The nurse heard her talking to Morgan and said, "She's lucky. She could have hit an artery, and it would've been a lot worse. You really ought to get her some help. It's a shame kids are turning to this," the nurse said in a judgmental tone.

Morgan's mother looked at her and said, "Look, you witch, don't you have anything else to do besides bother us? If I want your advice, I'll ask for it. We're handling this as a family and don't need your input. By the way, what's your name?"

"I'm sorry, ma'am. I didn't mean any harm."

"My child is sixteen years old, and she can hear your negativity. You don't know us. You really need to have some sensitivity training. I'm going to speak with your superiors."

The nurse apologized and quickly left. Morgan's mother continued comforting her. Her father walked into the room. He was worried; he felt helpless. He had hoped that it was just a phase, and it seemed they were dealing with it, and Morgan appeared to be getting better; he realized that this would take more time than he thought. He comforted her. His heart sank when he saw her body.

The doctor spoke to them about her condition. Her parents informed the doctors they were getting help for her. They gave them Dr. Callahan's information so they could contact him. They discussed what sent her over the edge. Her friends had given them the flyers. The police were called to the hospital, and they took the flyers and began an investigation into where they came from. Because Morgan was well-liked by all her peers, the only suspect was her disgruntled ex-boyfriend.

Morgan had to stay at the hospital for observation. After a seventy-two-hour stay, she was released into her parents' care. Morgan hated the hospital and was relieved to be back with her parents. When they arrived home, Munsey had lunch prepared for them. Her parents comforted her and had a family discussion about the flyers.

Her father said, "Angel, let's talk about this. What's been done to you is a cruel, sick prank. We're going to find the person who did this to you, although I have my suspicions. I must tell you, I'm upset about this, too. When someone hurts you, they hurt us as well. I understand why you're upset. I know this is devastating to you. You gave us a scare. Your mother and I would be devastated if you didn't make it through this. We're concerned about your safety and your well-being. Please talk to us. Let us know how we can help you. What can we do, as your parents, to keep you from injuring yourself? We need to know how we can help you."

Her mother interrupted, "Open up sweetie. Talk to us. We want to help you."

Holding her injured arm, Morgan looked at her parents and said, "It's difficult to explain. Sometimes, when I'm hurting, I hide and cut. I feel extremely alone in that moment. It feels like no one else knows my pain. Nobody understands what it's like to hurt in the worse way possible. I don't want to spoil the mood of anyone around me. I don't want anyone to feel sorry for me, and I feel nobody can help me in that moment. Cutting is the only remedy. It's like the only thing that actually helps."

"How can something so painful help? Don't you feel the pain of the cut?" her mother asked, trying to gain a better understanding of what was going on with her child.

"Mom, I can't explain it. It's like this high. The pain instantly goes away, and afterward, I feel better."

"Why not come to us?" her mother asked.

"I know you want to help, but there is absolutely nothing you can do for me at the time I'm experiencing pain. You don't understand, and you probably never will. I was devastated about the flyers. If I had come to you, what could you have done to dull the pain? I cut so I won't have to feel the emotional pain."

Her dad touched her shoulder and looked at her face to face, "Angel, that's extremely dangerous. Your wounds could have gotten infected, and lord knows what else could happen to you."

"What else can I do? I felt alone. How else can I make the pain go away?" she asked.

"That's what Dr. Callahan is going to show us. If we can find a way to help you, will you try Angel?"

Morgan saw the worry and pain in her parents. She saw the tears in her mother's eyes. Her eyes were swollen from her crying all night and worrying about her. She didn't know how much pain she was causing until that moment. Her parents' desperate plea made her want to try. She wanted to be better, if not for herself, at least for their sakes. Rarely did she see her parents so distraught, and she hated that she was the cause of their pain. She knew she had to stop cutting, but how? She didn't know, but she felt determined to give it a try. She looked at her father and said, "Dad, I'll try."

Dr. Callahan saw her three times a week, and she was put into group therapy with others. Her best friend Mackenzie wanted to be a part of her healing process, so she visited every day. Weeks passed, and Morgan was getting better. She looked forward to therapy sessions and was making new friends. School was in session, and her friends received her with warmth. They let her know that they didn't condone what happened to her and that they were there for her if she needed them. All was well.

Getting Prepared

The twelfth-grade social studies class of Holbrook High School was gearing up for their trip to Barcelona, Spain, in the next month. Since they had two weeks out for spring break, the trip was planned for that time. Morgan and her friends had been shopping for the trip. They would be there for seven days. It was Saturday morning, and the girls were at Mackenzie's house on the internet, looking up places to dine and shop upon their arrival. Morgan's mother called her home. She immediately left. She went inside and found her mother who had just gotten dressed.

"Morgan, your Aunt Edy and I are taking you shopping for your trip." Morgan smiled.

"Sounds like fun. I've already bought so much. I may not be able to carry all the stuff I already have, but I'm not going to turn down a shopping trip."

"I didn't think you would mind." They both laughed. Morgan got her purse and hopped in the car with her mother. As they were backing out of the driveway, she thought she saw Logan in their neighbor's yard. "Mom, did you see that?" She looked again, but there was nobody there. "It's nothing," she said, and she sat back in her seat. Logan was spending time in the juvenile detention center for the assault charges. He wasn't scheduled to be out for a while. She reasoned in her mind that she was just imagining things. They shopped until late in the evening. When they arrived home, they noticed that Morgan's car had been vandalized. All her windows were broken, and her tires were flattened. Her mother looked at the damage. "Who in the world would do something like this?"

Morgan immediately said, "Logan did this. I thought I saw him in the Harris' yard as we were leaving."

"No Morgan, Logan is still locked up."

They notified the police. Since there were no witnesses to the vandalism, they could only write a report. Morgan was afraid. She was on edge. She was suspicious of every sound she heard. She thought she heard someone knocking at her bedroom window, but each time she looked out, she didn't see anyone. She had her father check, but he didn't find anything. Morgan's parents went to bed. She wanted to chat with her friends, so she got online. She got a message from an unknown sender. The profile didn't have a picture in it, and she was almost certain the name Romeo was a fake one. The message read, "This is Romeo. I will find you Juliet and we shall die together." She immediately blocked the person. The person continued coming back in the form of other profiles. She finally closed her account and tried to go to sleep. She was startled when her cell phone rang then it stopped. It rang again then suddenly stopped. She picked it up to check the caller ID. It rang again and this time it continued ringing. It was an anonymous caller. She heard a raspy voice on the other end that said, "Hello Juliet. Are you ready to die?" She was afraid. Her body began to tremble. She didn't want to wake her parents, but she felt she had to. She remembered their talk with her. They insisted that she come to them when she was having problems. She went into their bedroom and saw they were sound asleep. She turned her phone off and lay in the chaise lounge next to the foot of their bed. She tried to go to sleep but her thoughts kept her awake. Although she didn't wake her parents, she felt much safer in their room. At last, she dozed off, but the family was awakened by the doorbell ringing. It was four-thirty in the morning. "Now who in the world could be at the door at this time of the morning?" her father asked. He sprinted from the bed and ran to the door. Morgan and her mother followed. Morgan was afraid. She didn't want her father to open the door. He looked through the peephole and saw it was the police department.

The male officer asked, "May we step inside?" Her dad said, "Sure officer come on in. What seems to be the problem?"

"We've got a report from the fire department that there's been a fire at Claire's Boutique. They're reporting major damages. We came by to let you know." Her mother said, "You mean my store has been set afire?"

"I'm sorry ma'am. They need you down there right away." Her mother was quite upset by the news. The officer left, and Morgan's parents got dressed. "Morgan, you stay here with Munsey," her father said. They left for the boutique. Munsey couldn't go back to sleep because of all the excitement. She decided to get an early start on doing chores. Morgan helped her because she too found it difficult to sleep. She was worried that it was Logan who set her mother's shop on fire. He told her that he would do it. First, her car gets damaged, and now her mother's shop. Morgan was sure of his involvement. After they were done cleaning the kitchen, Munsey said, "Thank you, Morgan. Can I bother you to take the trash to the curb for me?"

"Sure, no problem."

"I'll get breakfast started while you do that. Your parents should be home any minute now."

It had been a couple of hours since her parents left, and they hadn't heard any word from them about the fire. Morgan gathered the two small bags of trash and took them outdoors. The sun had yet to come up. It was eerily quiet out. Birds weren't chirping, nothing moved, not even the wind, not a sound. She felt as though she was being watched. She thought she heard rustling in the bushes. She immediately stopped in her tracks. She studied the bushes for a second. It was nothing. She proceeded to the trash can. She flipped the lid and threw one bag inside and went for the other. As she was putting the trash in the can, someone grab her arm. She felt what seemed to be a gun in her side. She looked up to see who the culprit was. It was Logan. He looked at her with eyes she didn't recognize and said, "Hello Juliet, I told you I'd be coming for you.

Now if you scream, I will shoot you right here in this driveway, then after I'm done with you, I'll kill Munsey and then myself. Do you want that?" With a look of terror on her face, she shook her head. He walked her to his car which was parked down the street. He pushed her inside on the driver's side, then he got in the car keeping the gun pointed at her. He drove to his home which was a large posh estate. He took her to the guest house so his parents couldn't interfere, and he locked the door behind them.

In the meantime, Munsey was calling Morgan's name, but she didn't answer. She looked outside to see if she was still out there, but she saw no sign of her. Thinking that she was in her bedroom, she went there, and again, she saw no sign of Morgan. After looking for her with no results, she tried calling her cell phone, but it went straight to voicemail because the phone was off. She turned the power on and looked for Mackenzie's number. She found it and called her. Mackenzie was still asleep, so she didn't answer. She walked down to her place and rang the doorbell. Mackenzie's father came to the door.

"May I help you?"

"Yes, I wanted to know if Morgan came down here."

"Nobody's here, Mackenzie is still asleep. We haven't seen Morgan since yesterday."

"Are you sure?"

"Yes, I'm sure. I set the alarm last night and I had to deactivate it for you. Nobody's been in or out of here since last evening. She's not here, but if you'd like, I can ask my daughter if she knows where she may be." He let her inside and he went to wake his daughter. She had no clue where Morgan was. Her father relayed that message to her. Munsey left and hurried back to the house hoping Morgan had shown up. There was still no sign of her, so she called her parents.

"Mrs. Foster, have you heard from Morgan?"

"No, I haven't. We left her with you."

"Has she called you?"

"No, she hasn't. What's going on?" She took out the trash and I haven't seen her since. I looked around the home and I went to Mackenzie's place, and they haven't seen her either."

"Oh my god! Call the police we're on our way" She grabbed her husband by the arm who was still speaking with the fire chief. "Peter, Morgan's missing."

"What do you mean Morgan's missing?"

"Munsey just called and said she can't find her." Her parents rushed home. The police were already there taking Munsey's statement. They combed the area but there was no sign of her. They put out a missing child alert. Pretty soon everyone was looking for her. Her

96

mother was distraught. She was thinking that Morgan went somewhere and hurt herself critically. She rocked back and forth in her seat. The police and detective questioned her parents. They told her about her problem. They gave any information they deemed important to find her. Initially, her parents thought the fire at the boutique may have sent her over the edge. The police continued their investigation into her where-a bouts.

CHAPTER FIVE

Morgan was being held against her will by her deranged ex-boyfriend. He pushed her onto the sofa. She looked around the large room and noticed he'd built a shrine to her. Pictures of her were all over the place. She was astonished at the number of photos he had of her. She could tell by looking at some of the photos, that he had been stalking her for almost two years, long before they began dating. There were pictures of her with her parents, friends, and trips to the malls. He even had pictures of her in her latest stage performances and the most private moments in her life. Just about anywhere she was, he had been there. She had no idea how obsessed he was with her. In the beginning, she thought it was great that he liked her. She loved that he showered her with love and gifts. She was the center of his attention. She thought it was normal for a guy to like her the way he did. She had no idea she was dating an unstable stalker.

When the abuse started, it was early in the friendship. It was difficult to recognize at first. It started as emotional abuse, with him telling her how to wear her hair making subtle remarks about her appearance; how she looked unattractive in certain clothes, and certain hairstyles. She thought that since he truly liked her, perhaps he knew what was best for her. She began to see herself in his image of beauty for her. To please him, she did as he requested. The more she complied, the more he demanded until she had completely lost herself in him. She found it difficult to please him, although she tried. He became more and more abusive. She took his abuse and yelling as a sign of rejection, and she couldn't handle it, so she began cutting.

He kept her on a rollercoaster ride of emotional trauma. She was partly afraid of him, but she felt sorry for him each time he would apologize. He convinced her he wouldn't hit her again. She always went back. She was isolated from her family and friends. He made her feel guilty for wanting to spend time with anyone other than him.

When they broke up, he couldn't take it. He was supposed to spend several months in a juvenile unit, but with his father's money, the sentence was cut in half, and he was allowed to go to a reform school for boys to keep his record clear. He served the allotted time. With his father's generous donation to the school, Logan was given the run of the place. The school told the courts that he was rehabilitated and that he had exhibited perfect behavior. He was allowed to leave with time served, and he didn't have to register as a sex offender.

When Logan was younger, his parents put him off on nannies who were sometimes abusive to him. When his parents found out about the abuse, they felt guilty and allowed him to run amuck. Logan's parents were older. They lacked the energy or drive to keep up with him and allowed him to do as he pleased. He was aggressive towards his parents, and they gave in to his every whim. He appeared to be the perfect young man in public, but he was a demon seed. He was cunning and deceitful. His parents were always away, which left him to his own devices. They figured at the age of seventeen, he didn't need monitoring.

Morgan was on the sofa trembling. Logan wasn't saying anything, which frightened her. She didn't know what he was thinking. He was setting up the television. He wanted them to watch videos of them when they were dating, which he put to their favorite music. He was drinking alcohol.

"Logan, what are you doing?"

"I want to relive the moments when we fell in love."

"Why don't you let me call my parents so they'll know I'm okay?"

"You know what, don't mention your parents to me right now. They're the reason you were taken away from me. We were happy together before they got the police involved. I knew you would come back to me. It was only a matter of time. I'm going to fix it where we can always be together, and no one will ever separate us again."

"What do you mean by that?"

"You'll see. Get undressed." She slowly took her clothes off. There was a wedding dress lying on the sofa next to her.

"Put it on," he demanded. She did as she was told. As she put on the gown, he got dressed in a tuxedo he'd purchased. Once she was dressed, he had her put on her veil. He put an audio recording of a wedding ceremony. This is your wedding day. I told you we would be married."

"It's not a real wedding," she said. "It's just a recording."

"It'll have to do. Now, when he gets to your part, recite the words." He proceeded to carry out the mock wedding, which included exchanging rings and a reluctant kiss from Morgan. She didn't know what to expect and she was unsure of what he would do next, but she cooperated as much as possible. She tried not to make him angry. She wanted to keep him calm so that perhaps he would allow her to leave. She was nice to him. She calmed him.

"You know Logan, I was very upset when we broke up. I missed you terribly." She kissed him and convinced him she was still in love with him.

"I love you, Morgan Sparks. No one will ever come between us again. We'll live together in paradise. Now that we're married, we'll make love then we'll fall asleep forever. He had two glasses of wine. After we make love, we'll drink this wine and fall asleep in each other's arms."

He kissed her again. He caressed her shoulders. She knew there was poison in the wine, and she would die with Logan if she couldn't get help. There was a loud knock at the door. Logan was startled. He exhaled out of frustration, "What do my parents want? I should've known they would spoil this perfect event." He aimed the gun toward her face and said, "Don't you say one word, or I'll shoot you." He went to the door and opened it without checking to see who was there. It was the police department.

"Logan Sparks, I'm Officer James Nelson of the Holbrook Police Department. We're looking for a young lady by the name of Morgan Foster. Have you seen her?"

"You mean Morgan Sparks. She's my wife now. We were married today."

Officer Nelson noticed he was wearing a tuxedo. He then thought he was dealing with a runaway teen because he could see Morgan in her wedding dress.

He said, "Her family is concerned about her. May I come in?" He tried to close the door, but when he saw Officer Nelson was going to come in anyway, he backed away. Although the police officer was there, Morgan wasn't in the clear yet. She didn't feel safe in the least. She knew Logan still had the gun, and she wouldn't say or do anything until he was in handcuffs. Logan slowly walked over to where Morgan was standing. The officer didn't notice Logan's gun because he had it hidden. When he saw Morgan in her wedding gown, he thought for a moment they had gotten married. Logan stood next to Morgan and placed the gun in her back where the officer couldn't see it.

"Morgan Foster, your parents are looking for you."

"Please go away," she said. Her body shifted sideways when she spoke. By then, the officer saw the gun.

"You should leave officer," Logan said.

"Mr. Sparks, you know I can't do that," he said.

"Yes, you can. If you don't, I'm going to shoot her."

"Why would you want to hurt the woman you love?"

"I'm tired of people telling us we can't be together. If we can't be together in life, then we're going to be together in the afterlife. There our love will last forever. We'll never be apart."

Logan moved Morgan over to where the wine was. The officer was keeping a watchful eye on them.

"Let her go, Mr. Sparks." He ignored the officer and reached for his wine with his right hand. He drank it. He handed Morgan her glass.

She looked in the glass and said, "Logan, I don't want to drink this; it's poisonous."

"Just drink it; you won't even taste it," he said, trying to force the drink on her.

She took the wine, put her lips to the glass, and pretended to drink it. She allowed the glass to slip out of her hand, catching Logan off guard. Officer Nelson saw his chance to move in. Morgan saw the officer moving towards them. She ran for the door. Logan saw what was happening and in a split second, he lifted his gun to try and shoot Morgan. The officer already had his weapon drawn and he fired, shooting the teen center mass. Logan fell to the floor. Officer Nelson called for backup and an ambulance. Morgan ran out the door screaming. The officer couldn't perform CPR on Logan because he was concerned for his own safety. He wasn't sure what type of poison he'd ingested. Once he secured Logan's weapon, another officer came in to assist him. They took the safety gear from their car and rendered aid to Logan, but it was of no use. He had already expired. A female officer was there, and she comforted Morgan. Her parents were notified that she was found safe. She was taken to the hospital as a precaution. When her family learned what happened to her, they were upset, especially her mother. She spoke with her husband in private.

"Peter, I'm concerned about Morgan relapsing. She's been through a lot. I must tell you, this is extremely hard for me to take, so I know it must be difficult for her. She went through this trauma, and she did it alone. That boy planned on killing our child and then killing himself. Can you imagine how that must've made our baby feel? Sitting alone in the presence of a potential killer who was about to take her life. I think I'm going to need to speak with someone about this too. I mean it's only so much a family can take. And where were that boy's parents? Why was he allowed to do so much harm to our family? The police said he served in a diversion program and was released early, putting our family at risk. The crazy part is, that they never felt the need to warn us that he was being released.

Morgan was examined by the emergency staff and questioned again by the police. She was informed at the hospital that Logan had died. She cooperated with them until she couldn't speak anymore. She shut down and asked for her parents. She was released, and they took her home. Morgan was silent on the ride home. Her parents didn't pressure her to talk. By bedtime, she still hadn't said anything. Her mother slept in her bed with her to comfort her.

Over the next few days, she wasn't feeling any better. It seemed as if the whole experience had taken a lot out of her emotionally, and she was finding it hard to connect with her feelings. She was seeing Dr. Callahan. He noticed she was suffering emotionally, so he prescribed anti-depressants to help her. He suggested that she spend forty-eight hours in a facility for her safety and he warned her parents that if she didn't get any better, he would have to admit her for even longer. Two weeks after the ordeal, Morgan was talking again, but she was still coping.

Mackenzie came around, which seemed to cheer her up a bit. Around the third week, they were discussing their trip to Spain, which seemed to cheer Morgan up even more.

Her mother noticed that she seemed to feel better when she discussed the trip. She was sure that Spain would be good for her and a great escape from her past. Her mother had an idea to get all her good friends together and allow them all to come over for a cookout or a pizza party. She made the plans and secretly invited them all over. Her Aunt Edith was there, which always caused her joy. When Morgan saw all her friends showing up and she saw her aunt and her father, she felt better; she was surrounded by family and friends. They scrolled the internet, looking at not only Spain but other travel destinations. Morgan was laughing and enjoying her day. Her mother was pleased to see her smiling again. It took a minute, but she was almost back to her normal self. She seemed to be feeling better. This was reported to Dr. Callahan. He was happy to know that she was doing a little better, but he secretly told her parents that she must remain in Holbrook for therapy rather than go to Spain with her friends. He was concerned with her being there without her parents or access to proper treatment. Her parents knew she would be devastated at the news. Seeing her so excited about the trip, they found it difficult to tell her. They came up with a remedy. They would all take the trip to Spain together, even her Aunt Edith. Dr. Callahan said that if Morgan does well in the coming days, he would sign off on it. After the doctor signed the release for her to go, her parents told her the news. They all went, and Morgan's troubles seemed to fade. No one dared bring it up. After the trip, Morgan came home and continued her therapy. The process of getting her life back on the right path was long, and sometimes difficult, especially when old memories would pop up. With her continuing on her path of healing and treatment, she grew stronger. Soon, she was instrumental in speaking with other teens who were suffering from what she had been going through. She gained a newfound freedom in helping others. She finished high school and graduated college with a degree in child psychology. She remained in Holbrook and continued her acting on the side. Morgan ultimately went on to live a happy and healthy life.

CONCLUSION

There are times when we come across people who bring harm into our lives. We want to be kind to others and that's okay. Manipulative people seek to take advantage of that kindness or what they perceive as our weakness. They try to force their will upon others who they think are less powerful than them. They insist that you give in to their demands. Sometimes, the threats are blatant, but sometimes, they're subtle. Bullies often use intimidation to gain an advantage over their victims. If you're asked to do something against your will, it's perfectly okay to say no. You're under no obligation to please anyone. If they use intimidation with physical violence or threats of bodily harm, it then becomes a crime and should be reported to the authorities. You can also reach out to an adult or someone you trust. If you can, immediately remove yourself from the situation. You are very special, and you deserve the best. Nobody has the right to intimidate you.

In the story, the character Morgan Foster chooses to deal with her pain in an unhealthy way by using SI or self-injury "cutting." Some teens try drugs or alcohol. Some even use sex as a remedy. There are various activities teens engage in as a means of coping. These self-destructive habits only worsen the problem. Seek professional help for your emotional or physical pain. Although the process may seem difficult, it's far better to get help, than suffer alone. You will find that someone cares for you. If you are in an abusive relationship, get out immediately. Have an adult or authority figure or even law enforcement to assist you. There is hope.

National Domestic Violence Hotline 1-800-799-7283 www.thehotline.org

Self-Injury Hot Line   1-800-334-HELP

ABOUT THE AUTHOR

Karen Coleman is an Arkansas native. She enjoys writing exciting and dramatic stories. A phenomenal author with a distinctive style, she has demonstrated a sensational talent for steering her readers through every line and page with eager anticipation.

Karen has published several novels in various genres. Readers have described her novels as riveting, fast-paced, and thrilling.

Her teen novels are insightful and empowering. As a mentor who has worked with teens for many years, Karen understands the social challenges they face, and she skillfully addresses those topics with a finesse that lends excitement, adventure, and encouragement.

 A self-proclaimed writer of fiction with an element of truth, Karen began penning her thoughts as a hobby. After many years of writing and encouragement from those around her, she began writing on a more intense level, eventually turning out several wonderful novels. She offers something for almost every reader, from her adult crime series to her teen books, there's something to be enjoyed by all. Her literary works have garnered much fanfare and have not only been enjoyed by her many readers; she's highly celebrated among her writing peers. Her books are meant to inspire, uplift, and entertain, leaving her audience asking for more.

Karen is also a playwright, actor, and former city council member. She's the mother of four and a Glam-ma of thirteen and counting. Her grandchildren affectionately call her Nana. She's also the proud mom of two rambunctious miniature schnauzers. When not writing or spoiling her grandbabies, she spends her time crafting, fishing, or enjoying a great barbecue.

Check out these other adolescent books by the author:

No Place for Emily Ann

Whatever Happened to I love you?

In the Wrong Game

Frozen Dreams